The woman had eyes like poison orchids, Hugo thought.

Hugo couldn't explain to his assistant, Miss Gorringe, exactly what bothered him about the mysterious woman he had met.

"Do you want me to gather any information?"

"Could you find her name?"

"I expect so."

He nodded. "Fine. Fine—do that."

When he had gone she picked up the telephone on her desk. In the next two hours she made thirteen calls, then left a note for Bishop before she went out.

Melody Carr. Seems like a pseudonym. Will try making appointment for you. You are correct. She is dynamite steeped in cyanide. Am going out to buy you a shroud.

ADAM HALL

Bishop In Check

HarperPaperbacks
A Division of HarperCollins*Publishers*

This is a work of fiction. The characters, incidents, and dialogues are products of the author's imagination and are not to be construed as real. Any resemblance to actual events or persons, living or dead, is entirely coincidental.

HarperPaperbacks *A Division of* HarperCollins*Publishers*
10 East 53rd Street, New York, N.Y. 10022

This book is published by arrangement with the author.

Cover photography by Herman Estevez

First HarperPaperbacks printing: January 1991

Printed in the United States of America

HarperPaperbacks and colophon are trademarks of HarperCollins*Publishers*

10 9 8 7 6 5 4 3 2 1

1st

MOVE

THE NIGHT Brain was killed, there had been rain.

It had come without warning, in the way that sends people diving under the trees, packing up their deckchairs, dodging into the shop doorways down Oxford Street and into the shelters round the park (the old-fashioned kind that are nothing to do with bombs). Quick, warm rain that fell softly, slaking the long parched summer day before dark came and it slept.

By midnight the sky was clear again from the Dogger Bank to the Scilly Isles, and half the moon was up there, queening it. By three in the morning the gleam had gone from roofs and pavements where there was lamplight, and dust was back in town; but in the country places the leaves were still greener for the rain, and where roads ran beneath trees there was still a puddle or two reflecting the moon.

A grey car moved, ghost-quiet through these early hours, and crossed the border into Surrey, heading for London. The clock on the dashboard said five past three. The speedometer turned up another nought as a signpost said South Knoll.

Bishop was cramped. He had driven through most of the day, and all of the night; now it was morning, and his eyes took longer to blink as the lamp-beams ahead of him raked the road, fading out a few hundred yards distant along a straight stretch, brightening swiftly against a curve, sometimes picking up the glint of eyes, the flit of wings.

Soon after South Knoll the road went dark. It had rained more here than in other places. The headlamp beams took on a yellow tinge; the hedges were greener; the tires hissed over the wet.

There were three gallons left on the gauge, and he began wondering if he could make London, or whether he should take the Dorking road, losing a few miles but filling the tank at the all-night garage there. In a little while he got bored with working out distances and m.p.g. and decided to risk it. The vintage Rolls-Royce fled softly through the moonlight; he felt it would take him far beyond London even with an empty tank: after three hundred miles this classic machine, sired by fabulous minds from English steel, had a mood of its own in the light of the moon, and petrol was a daytime thing to be ignored.

Going up the curve of Knoll Hill the car neared another. Lights were flushing down through the trees, brightening fast. Bishop pressed the dip-switch, but the other man did not. His lights were blinding, flooding the grey limousine and filling it with a clear white glow that blazed from all directions, striking even the mirror, bouncing there from the rear window.

Bishop sat trapped in the dazzle, jabbing the dipswitch twice, asking for manners. The other car just came on. When Bishop realized that something odd seemed to be cropping up he tucked in to his near side, using the last spare yard between his front fender and the chalk slope edging the road. This kept him out of actual trouble, but the other man was going into a fast slide now and he clipped paint off the rear fender of the limousine as he went past.

Bishop pulled up, right against the chalk slope. On the other side of the road there was a board fence, painted black and white to show up clearly. The cream-colored Ventura was going through that, breaking it up with a lot of noise.

Beyond the fence was a steep down-slope with trees. Bishop was getting out of his car as the Ventura dived into them, and as he began running across the road there was an impact that could only be final. Afterwards there was just silence, except for Bishop's feet.

He ran over the wet leaves and the white line and the smears made by the Ventura's tires. Glass lay like frost on the roadway near the broken fence. As he dived through the gap he wondered if he could get down there before anything caught fire, and at the same time wondered if it would matter. Nothing of the Ventura's weight could go through a fence this tough below seventy. A human, sitting in the middle of all that metal and timber, wouldn't have a chance.

He grazed his shin on a sawn off tree trunk as he ran down the slope of earth; it was dark and fibrous and laced with bramble. A tin can clanked as his foot caught it and he flung out a hand to stop stunning himself against a low bough.

Farther down and to the left was the dark shape of the car. It was wedged like a dead elephant between two trees in the faint cold light of the moon. Even in the grunt of his own breath and the sliding thud of his feet Bishop knew how silent it would be down here among the trees, if it weren't for the sounds he made.

The light threw queer patterns, the crisscross of bough shadows and the mottle of leaves. It touched the rim of the wheel that was still turning, the near-side front wheel that still had a little energy left. The car was on its side.

When Bishop had looked at the driver he straightened up and stood back, for some odd reason watching the front wheel. In this quiet place he and it were the only two things that moved. It spun more and more slowly and there was the faint grating of a cracked roller-bearing. His eyes, focusing on a small gleam—moonlight on a wet leaf—beyond the rim of the tire, saw that the wheel was out of line. For another minute the distorted segment of it dipped ... dipped ... dipped against the gleam of the leaf as the wheel turned. When at last it stopped, optical reaction sent it moving back very slowly the other way. Then gradually even the mirage of movement died, and the thing was still.

While he had stood there, sounds had come down from the road. A car had gone by at speed, then had slowed, as if the driver had seen the break in the fence and the frost of glass. Gears meshed now; the engine raced in reverse and

the transmission whined. The car stopped. The
engine died. A door slammed. Quick footsteps
echoed in the arch of leaves.

Bishop looked at the chassis of the wreck. It
was exposed, like an animal pitched over dead.
A white sliver of wood, ripped from the fence,
was trapped between the clutch housing and a
cross-member. A tangle of briar had been caught
in a shackle and drawn back, its green tress fan-
ning out. One of the rear tires had burst, wrap-
ping round the brake drum, choking it. Fumes
rose from the hot rubber, sickly on the air. Oil,
glinting black in the moonlight, had begun to
creep from a split in the axle casing, and in
a moment it hung in a long gleaming tendril
from there to the earth. The silencer was ripped
and flattened. Sump studs were streamered with
grass. A U-bolt had sheared clean. The hood
gaped open like a dead mouth.

Beyond the wreck someone was moving. The
pale blur of a face came nearer, jerkily as feet
slipped on the earth slope. Details grew more
distinct: loose dark hair, wink of a bracelet, the
dull crimson of lipstick.

Bishop heard the catch of breath as she almost
tripped and then steadied herself, to stand within yards of the smashed car, looking at him.

Liquid—either   water   or   gasoline—began

leaking somewhere. The small sound splashed into the quietness, on to the soft earth. The intervals between the drips shortened, the *pit-pit-pit* quickening, faster and faster until they became an unbroken stream and there was steady silence.

Bishop said: "There's nothing we can do."

"How do you know?"

She moved towards the car, so he went round quickly and stood between it and her. She looked up into his face and said again:

"How do you know?"

With a movement he persuaded her to turn away from the wreck.

"You must take my word for it."

For a time she stood perfectly still, looking down at her shoes. The smell of gasoline came in the air. The leak was from the tank, not the radiator.

Bishop watched the woman. She was young, slim, expensive. She had forgotten he was here. She had the stillness of the Sphinx. Then she raised her head suddenly and went forward, climbing the slope. It was not easy, in the high heels. Bishop caught up with her and helped her over the worst places where there was a lot of bramble and where the dark moist earth was steep. Once when she slipped he steadied her;

7

on this warm night her hand was like dry ice.

They reached the top, and the gap in the fence. She turned round, looking down into the trees. In a moment she said in a flat negative tone:

"I knew him."

Bishop looked at her.

"Yes?" Her stillness was absolute. "I'm sorry—"

She turned and they walked through the gap to the roadway. He said: "I'll go and phone the police. There's a phone booth at the bottom of the hill."

While he was speaking she walked away with quick, light steps, and got into her car. The door slammed and she started the engine. With a neat turn across the roadway she drove off, up the hill. As she reached the curve the red tail lights flicked out. The sound of the engine died. Bishop thought it was all rather odd.

When he had been to the telephone booth he drove back slowly to the gap in the fence, switched off and sat waiting. They were here within minutes: a sweep of lights, a rising engine-note, the streep of tires over the wet leaves. A Wolseley with two policemen. They parked a few yards behind the grey limousine.

Click of the door latches; footsteps: "Mr. Bishop?"

He said yes, and got out of the car. As they climbed through the fence an ambulance came up, looking very luxurious with polished cream finish and quiet quite lights burning inside. Bishop went down the slope with the two policemen. Leavings of rain still came dripping from the arch of leaves, enormous tears that stung when they hit.

Down at the bottom, the two men looked at the driver of the smashed Ventura. Bishop watched their faces. One of them screwed up his eyes a fraction. The other's expression did not change. He might have been looking at any ordinary thing, something quite wholesome.

The ambulance crew came down, and the policemen started using tape measures. While Bishop was giving them a brief statement they heard a wrecking crane arrive on the hill road. Soon afterwards a beam of light came slanting down through the trees, playing on the wreck. In its glow their faces looked paler.

A voice sounded, up on the road. Someone began sweeping the glass away by the hole in the fence. It reminded Bishop of a long time ago, of a tired waiter clearing up the glass from a maple floor just about this hour of a morning. The tinkling rhythm of this broom on the roadway was much the same, slow and philosophical, brushing aside the thought that this wasn't the last of the broken glass in the world: tomorrow there'd be more: these bright splinters were the by-product of a society.

When he had made his statement Bishop went up the slope. The ambulance crew had already climbed it, taking their stretcher and the thing under the blanket. On the hill some other people had arrived and were measuring tire marks. It was all very quiet and efficient: a few figures being called in low voices; the winding of tape measures into their cases; the flash of a torch; the glow of a cigarette; a cough. While Bishop stood there he heard the men puzzling about something. Words were called: "Firestone" ... "Dunlop" ... "Michelin" ... "turned just here." He realized what their trouble was, and went up to one of them.

"Mine are the Dunlops. I don't know about his. The third set belong to a Delage—French—so they could be the Michelins. It came down the hill, stopped, backed up to the fence here. Then it turned across the road and went up the hill."

They nodded and did a careful recheck, seeming more satisfied. The wrecking crane was turning; chain links rattled as the heavy clutch shuddered under the load. It was going away without shifting the wreck; that was probably a daylight job. The ambulance had gone off a long time ago. People were packing up. Bishop got into his car and moved away up the hill, changing his mind about gasoline and taking the Dorking road.

At the garage, while the tank was being filled, he looked at the rear fender that the other car had struck. Damage was light; the fender was only skinned, and a streak of cream paint had been left on the graze. Waiting for change, he thought about the grey Delage and the woman. He would have liked to know why she had gone off like that, leaving him three words that had been spoken more to herself than to him, and why she had turned the car, going the way she had come.

She had said she knew the man in the wreck. They might have been traveling together, in convoy. Her way was his; he had stopped; all she could do was go back; wherever they had been going did not matter anymore.

Bishop stopped thinking, and drove home. He reached there at five o'clock. He unstuck the sock from the graze on his shin and took a cold shower to drain all the distance away. It was already dawn, so he drew the curtains across and lay on the bed, trying to sleep. After three hundred and fifty miles his body was tingling

11

tired, but his brain was clear and sleep wasn't available.

There was too much to think about: not about the evidence he had seen of how grotesque the human form could be made by violence, not about the potential head-on smash that he had managed to reduce to a grazed fender, but about the woman. The chill of her hand when he had stopped her tripping; the calm of her voice when she had said she knew him; the way she had just driven off.

And her eyes. Intense blue in a face not quite attractive, just a setting for the eyes. They had been wide and cold and quiet when she had looked at him across the wreck. There had been no shock in them, no pity and no pain.

Sleep would not have come to Bishop anyway, because daylight was on the curtains and he hadn't the knack of cats. But even if it had been dark, she would have kept it away.

2*nd*

MOVE

MISS GORRINGE was dusting the desk. It was a very large limed oak desk that took thirty minutes to dust every morning: or three minutes to dust and the rest of the time to take everything off it and put everything back: the ivory telephone, a stack of magazines months high, the sandalwood cigarette box, Chinese jade figurines, tobacco bowl, ash bowl, pipe rack, writing paper, cactus plant, boxes of matches, paper knives, books, blotters, note pads, pencils, sealing wax, candlesticks, glass paper-weights, a lump of moist clay. . . . She looked at the lump of moist clay. It was new.

Almost every morning there was something new. Yesterday, Bishop has met Clifford Moor, who had given him the clay. In Moor's hands it had been an unworked masterpiece, material for genius. In Bishop's hands it was a lump of clay and would always be. But he would try to mould it into a figure before he threw it at something and gave up being a sculptor. Tomorrow he would meet Strokorsky and there'd be a cello on the desk, or he'd meet a bricklayer and there'd be a bucket of cement and a trowel.

Miss Gorringe was, of course, exaggerating to herself as she replaced the magazines beside the telephone; but there had actually been a morning when she had found a deep-sea diver's helmet on this desk. Bishop had bought it at an auction because he said he was interested in fish. He had spent the day burnishing the copper and putting it on his head and peering about the place like a drunken somnambulist. It was a jardinière now, inverted and suspended and full of geraniums in the little walled garden at the back.

Miss Gorringe was holding the lump of clay and sniffing its pleasant half-built-house smell when Bishop came into the room. It was seven o'clock, but he was dressed.

She looked at him and said quietly:

"Your watch is fast. It's still night."

He wandered vaguely about the room with his hands behind him. She sighed gently and watched him, trying to name his mood. He had a variety of moods, all different and no rubbish. They were quiet ones, every time. Sometimes infuriatingly quiet. This one was easy to tag. It was the familiar Static Restlessness. Something had happened during the night.

"What's happened," she asked, "during the night?"

Bishop watched her put the Chinese jade water-carrier next to the pipe bowl, the lump of clay on the blotting pad. Trust Gorry to be on to something like this, within twelve hours of the event. He remembered a year ago, when she had come into this room and slapped a cablegram on his desk: *Woman's lacquered fingernails found in stomach of dead shark off Teneriffe. Interest Bishop?* A month afterwards a ship's steward was arrested in Cape Town, and Bishop came back to file the facts in his case book: a murder had lost perfection because the shark had kept the evidence; but Gorry had found him the job. Middle-aged and conservative, with a taste for embroidery and an Oxford degree, Vera Gorringe had a fantastic flair for nosing out the fantastic, the incredible and the macabre.

He came wandering over to the desk, putting his hands on its edge and peering among the bric-a-brac for his meerschaum pipe. While he was filling it he murmured without looking up: "I like that smock. It's a honey."

"Thank you, Hugo." She moved across the room to the Bechstein with her duster. It was a flow-ered smock, found yesterday in a back street market where its value had not been guessed. It was Burmese silk and had cost five shillings. The man had called it an "apron." She felt mean, buying it.

She said: "What did you do with the car? It's chipped."

He was sitting in the carved chair behind his desk, tilted back and watching the sunlight that dwelled in a Victorian glass paperweight.

"That was a ricochet."

"Whose fault?"

"The other fellow's."

E flat sounded in the room as she dusted the keyboard.

"Did you get his number?"

"Yes."

She closed the lid and picked up a flower vase to take it out.

"I hate to see chips on your chariot. Sue him good."

When she came back in half an hour she found him still sitting in the chair looking vague.

"Have you had any breakfast, Hugo?"

"M'm?"

Gently she said: "Break-fast. An-y. Have you had?"

"No."

She went out. He was in the Deep Trance (Occasional, Usually after Late Nights). Like that, he was part of the furniture. If he were still like that at lunch time, she would give him a quick rub over with the duster and leave him until tomorrow morning.

He was still like that at lunch time, but she had a midday paper with her as she came in, and risked disrupting his séance.

"Hugo."

"M'm?"

"This man Brain." She sat behind her own desk. It was against the wall at right angles to his, twelve feet distant. It was so unlike his in its order and efficiency that it was hardly possible to give the same name to both pieces of furniture.

"Who?" he asked. Ash dropped from his meerschaum on to his trousers. He carefully brushed it in.

"David Brain. The deceased."

"I don't know him," he said irritably. "And it sounds too late now."

She read from the paper.

In the early hours of this morning a Ventura car skidded from the road down Knoll Hill, Surrey, and crashed into the trees. The only occupant was its driver, David Brain, 35, a company director. He was killed outright. The police were summoned to the spot—one of the most dangerous hills in Southeast England—by a motorist whose car was slightly damaged by the skidding Ventura as it plunged off the road. This is the seventh accident on Knoll Hill this year, and the second fatality.

When she had stopped, Bishop said:

"Ah. So that's his name. I didn't know."

"Is this what you've been brooding about all the morning, Hugo?"

"I suppose it is, yes." His voice became less vague. "But for no reason, really. It just looked like a straight accident."

"Don't you think it was?"

"I've no reason to think otherwise. No reason to think about it at all." He touched an ornament on the desk, watching it reflect the sunlight. "But it was one of those things that seemed to have odd bits sticking out. How did you connect it with me?"

"Knoll Hill was on your route home. The time

18

was right. Your fender was chipped. You *were* the motorist who fetched the police?"

"Yes."

He got up and began walking about. He told her what had happened on the hill. There was silence for a few minutes, then Miss Gorringe said:

"It's the woman who interests you."

"That's right."

"What's she like, in more detail?"

"Fierce. Cold fierce. I don't know how well she knew this man—Brain—?"

"David Brain."

"But even if he'd been a complete stranger I would have expected her to show more shock than she did. There was a lot going on inside, but nothing in the eyes."

"What was there in the eyes?"

"Sex."

Vera Gorringe looked up.

"Sex?"

"Nothing else. I don't think there's room for anything else."

"You don't mean she gave you the come-hither at the actual graveside?"

He picked up a book and looked at it.

"Oh, no. Just eyes like poisoned orchids, you know? Flecked and deep. A nympho's eyes."

Carefully Miss Gorringe said: "If she'd worn galoshes and pince-nez, would you still be so interested in this crash?"

He dropped the book and stood balanced on the edge of his shoes.

"No. I don't think the crash would have happened if she'd been like that. Women like that have different backgrounds. You see what I mean, Gorry?"

"You mean this kind of girl is found in that kind of place."

"That's right. A nympho goes about like an unexploded bomb, and men get so excited running like hell or trying to take the fuse out that things happen to them." He looked down at Miss Gorringe reflectively. "I wish you'd been there. Atmospheres are difficult to absorb at second hand. If you like you can just say I'm stuck on a siren and trying to work up a mystery. I wouldn't blame you."

Miss Gorringe shook her head.

"Not you. You've got sensitive antennae, and when they wave about in atmosphere they don't make mistakes." She began cutting out the report of Brain's crash. "But isn't it like you? You can't get grazed by a drunk or a learner-driver; it has to be a man who goes about with a woman like this. Both going like blazes through the night."

She reached behind her for a file, and clipped the cutting in. "If this turns into a case, Hugo, it'll be the first time you've run into one personally and by chance. That's refreshing."

"Yes." He wasn't listening.

"Do you want me to gather any information?"

"M'm?"

"In-form-ation. You want?"

He went wandering back to his desk.

"I don't know, Gorry."

For a long time she was quiet. She knew he was poking about down there among the trees where the crashed car was, sniffing for smells, listening for inflexions in the woman's voice, watching her face, remembering small things that would have faded and become blurred by tomorrow if he didn't catch them now and fix them in their fresh colors. He wasn't in this room. He was back in Surrey with a kind of butterfly net and a killing bottle, hunting impressions on the wing.

He got up again so suddenly that she was startled.

"Information on what?" he asked actively.

"David Brain, his past. The woman, who she was—"

"Could you find her name?"

"I expect so."

He nodded. "Fine. Fine—do that."

"It won't be easy, Hugo. I can't concentrate
while you're running hot and cold all round the
room. Could you just go out and have lunch
somewhere far away? Say Cornwall?"

"I've just got back from there."

He opened the door. She called:

"Keep some time free. I might be able to find
out where you can meet her. You'd like to see
her again?"

"Yes."

When he had gone she picked up the telephone on her desk. In the next two hours she
made thirteen calls, then left a note for Bishop
before she went out.

*Melody Carr. Seems like pseudonym. Real
name probably Maggie Higgenbotham. Will
try making appointment for you. You are
correct. She is dynamite steeped in cyanide.
Am going out to buy you a shroud.*

In the afternoon Bishop slept four hours. Miss
Gorringe was still out when he woke. She came
back just before ten o'clock and found a note:
Copacabana. She telephoned the restaurant. Mr.
Bishop had left five minutes ago for home. She
waited.

When he came in she said:

"I can't arrange an introduction, Hugo. But she's at Romero's now, if you'd like to look in there."

"I'm not a member."

"Teddy Winslow would take you in."

"When?"

"As soon as you telephone him."

He said: "You're magic."

"No, just hard working."

"How did you find her?"

"I rang all the rakes in town."

He smiled slowly. "A nice angle. But I wouldn't have called Teddy a rake."

She said: "How little you know about your friends. Are you going?"

"Yes. I've done too much thinking, about the crash. I've begun imagining things, just to make the pattern fit." He picked up his telephone. "What's the situation, Gorry?"

"There are no complications. Someone is at Romero's whom you'd like to meet. Teddy would be glad to take you as his guest, but the bill is yours. He's just broken his airplane again and is living on sardines."

"How is his neck?"

"He didn't break that."

"How well does he know Melody Carr?"

"Scarcely at all—his own preference. He can't

introduce you, but I should think last night's little episode would stand your approaching the lady. She's apparently most approachable by elegant young gentlemen. Teddy says it would be like walking into a fire. I hope you have your asbestos bodice on."

She left him to ring Winslow.

Winslow was waiting for him on the top step of the Skyhigh Club, big and broad and red faced. When Bishop opened the near side door of the car he got in and settled down like a boar in a water hole.

"I knew you wouldn't want to come in," he said with a cheerful grin.

The Skyhigh Club was a tatty little place full of unpresentable débutantes and ex-R.A.F. officers. Bishop said tactfully:

"Well, they'll have heard the dramatic story of your air disaster, and you wouldn't have been able to tell it all over again to me in front of them. What happened?"

They drove down the Mall. Winslow said gloomily:

"Nothing. There weren't even any flames. I just ran out of fuel and lobbed down in a marsh. All I suffered was a mouthful of Essex ooze. They nearly drummed me out of the club. What the devil d'you want to meet this woman for?"

"She interests me."

"She interests most men. Absolute Superhet Sarah. But I shouldn't have thought she was quite your type."

They went along Grosvenor Street and into the Square. Halfway down Park Lane Bishop saw a gunmetal grey Delage parked outside Romero's.

"There's her car," Winslow said. "The Ritzy bauble in grey."

They got out of the ancient Rolls-Royce.

"Yes," said Bishop.

"You know it?"

"Yes. I saw her in it last night." As they walked into the club he asked: "You know a man called David Brain?"

Winslow said he had met him once.

"He was killed, early this morning."

Winslow studied his face carefully.

"What an odd cove you are, Hugo. Wherever you go there's a faint smell of coffins. The last time I had dinner with you a big man in boots came sliding in and said someone called Simpson or Thompson had been dredged out of the Thames, and you had to go off and identify the remains, halfway through our cigars."

"Well, I apologized."

"That's not the point. I've never quite found out what you do for a living, but I'm beginning to

25

suspect you're a high-class undertaker's tout."

They sat down at a table on the dais. It was Monday and there weren't many people here. A small Latin band was playing in a contented sort of way like a man humming to himself. Bishop's back was against the wall and he could see nearly everyone here.

"What shall we drink?" asked Winslow. His pudgy face was brooding. He had started out to bring Bishop within reach of a notorious nymphomaniac; now there seemed to be a death involved somewhere; the night had grown more serious. Winslow preferred it that way; but it made him broody about the face.

"I don't think I mind," said Bishop.

"Well, I've been on brandies."

"All right, let's have brandy."

Winslow ordered a bottle and they lit cigarettes. He said: "Where is she?"

Bishop looked past his left shoulder.

"Over there. Sitting alone."

Winslow moved round very slowly, hooking his arm over the back of the chair.

She was at a small table on the far side of the band. On the table was a glass and a small jeweled handbag. She was quietly tearing a slip of writing paper into pieces, very slowly and reasonably and methodically, across and across.

When the wad was too thick to tear she divided it, and took each half in turn, until the pieces were not much larger than confetti.

She put them into an ash tray and shut the handbag and looked up as if she had just remembered she wasn't alone in here.

In a few minutes Winslow looked back at Bishop with his face studiously blanked and asked: "Tell me about Brain getting killed."

A bottle arrived. Winslow half-filled their glasses. He said: "What about some ginger ale?" Bishop nodded, so they asked for some.

"He skidded off a road," Bishop said, "and I stopped to help. That girl came along."

"Was Brain killed outright?"

"Yes."

Winslow cupped the glass in his hand, watching the pale imprint of his palm through the brandy.

Bishop was watching the woman. She had a peacock blue dress on that showed her shoulders. They were lean and she had spent a lot of time in the sun.

Winslow said with a frown: "I do agree she's a bit odd, Hugo. Not many women would come in here alone and sit and drink alone."

"She might be waiting for someone."

"Well, then he would have met her outside or

27

somewhere else, and brought her in. Besides, does she *look* as if she's waiting for anyone?"

"No," said Bishop. He felt annoyed with Winslow. He wanted to think, and watch the woman.

"What's the connection between her and Brain?"

"She told me she knew him."

"Very well?"

"I don't know," said Bishop. "But I've a feeling she did."

Winslow swung his round red face to watch the room again. "Even if she only knew him a little, she's not exactly in deep mourning. I'd have said she was here to celebrate something, quietly getting squiffed, all by herself."

"Perhaps that's just what she's doing," said Bishop.

They sat for ten minutes without another word. Bishop was able to study the girl. Winslow finished two more brandies and began to feel loosened up. He hadn't been drinking very much since the plane crash two months ago, because it wasn't a marsh he had hit, it was a cattle shed, and the Proctor had caught fire while he was trying to drag his enormous frame out of the caved in cockpit and the smashed roof. There had been cows there; they did a lot of bellowing.

Winslow had smashed his way clear of the blaze and did his best to help the farm hands get the beasts out. They freed five. Two were roasted.

Winslow hadn't told his friends. Those who had seen the four lines in the papers couldn't get more than a grunt out of him. The others, like Bishop, believed he came down in a marsh. Winslow didn't want to talk about the fire, about the cows. He liked cows; they were gentle. Their bellowing, just the sound of it coming out of that mass of flame, would torment him for a long time. These nights he dreamed about the trumpets of terror, and the way, suddenly, they'd stopped.

He poured one more brandy each and said:

"Go across and introduce yourself, Hugo. Isn't that why I brought you here?"

Bishop didn't say anything. He was chasing a line of thought. Winslow knew he might as well just talk to himself all the time there was the dough mask over that lean chiseled face. Reflectively he murmured, "You can't do this to me. If she'd been at Tulio's or the Golden Moon you'd have asked Bob Leach or Tony Cox, and I wouldn't have known you were back in town until I saw your name in the Police Gazette. But here we are and there she is. The irresistible force has been—been brought into contact with

29

the immovable—immovable what?"

"Object."

Winslow swung his huge, handsome head up.

"So you're listening. . . . " He looked seriously at Bishop. "This is my last brandy. I don't want to get bingo. Something might happen. There are two components of a bomb in here tonight, and any moment they're liable to merge. I want to be sober enough to appreciate the percussion."

Bishop smiled. He liked Winslow. He wanted to ask him about the marsh, how the burn scar had got on his left wrist; but he knew it was no good; Winslow always backed his lies to the hilt.

Bishop said: "There'll be no explosion, Teddy."

"But I'm relying on you."

"I'm unreliable."

Winslow shook his head and lit another cigarette.

"I've seen you with the pin out before, and I'm just counting ten. Then I'll duck."

Bishop looked past his left shoulder, over the knuckles of his own clasped hands.

She was sitting there looking at nothing. The room might have been empty. Bishop thought that if everyone suddenly left the wall seats and the tables and the dance floor and went out, Melody Carr would go on sitting there with her lean, tanned shoulders and her glass and the tiny pile of torn-up paper in the ash tray. She wasn't seeing the lights, hearing the music, touching the table, aware of the warmth. No friend would come in. No one would speak to her, disturb her, break into that small reign of quietness over there. She had shut herself up in a private room with invisible walls, and the door was locked.

After what seemed a long time Winslow said:

"What was the first word she ever spoke to you?"

Bishop wondered what his thought train was. He said:

"She asked me how I knew Brain was dead."

"And how did you?"

"Sometimes death isn't subtle."

"Oh God, let's talk about Danny Kaye or Martha Raye. It can happen to anyone. One day it's going to happen to me. I had to get the pilot out of a Spit, once. He'd hit ground at full throttle and ninety degrees. Every night for months I woke up and couldn't get to sleep again. I just lay there and stared up in the dark at where I hoped to God the ceiling still was. You know?"

"Yes."

"If I have one more brandy, will I feel worse or better?"

"Than what?"

"Than now."

Bishop said nothing. Without any physical clue, he knew suddenly that in another moment she would turn her head and look this way. But she wouldn't really see him, any more than she had really seen him last night among the trees, because she was seeing Brain. Sitting there in this crowd, she was alone, out of this room, out of this world.

With deliberate consideration Winslow said: *"Better, I believe. . . ."* He gave himself another drink.

Bishop sat rigid. Her head was turning. She was looking across at the people on the dance floor. No, not looking *at* them, just looking their way.

He began waiting, watching the slow poised movement of her head. He had an odd feeling, as if he were a man in desperate hiding, waiting for the instant of discovery that was clearly to come, soon now.

She looked at the tables along the edge of the dais, beyond the little wrought-iron balustrade and the banked geraniums, her head turning this way by infinite degrees. The band started on *Jezebel*. A blue spotlight hit the microphone. An Italian in a white silk bandit's blouse began singing. Suddenly their eyes met, hers and Bishop's, across the bright glow of the flowers.

32

He was wrong. She was really seeing him.

"No," said Winslow, "I'm feeling worse. You've got me morbid, by telling me about. . . . " Bishop was not listening. The words were coming from the other side of something very far away. He didn't hear them, any more than he heard what the little Italian was singing.

She looked down suddenly at her hands. They were together on the table.

Bishop relaxed.

" . . . in here last week," Winslow's voice came, "with a Rank starlet. A very eye stopping model, you know? Six-cylinder hips and self change emotions. I was introduced."

Bishop looked at him.

"Yes?" he said. Winslow nodded. He said in a soft, slow, serious tone:

"I've never got over beautiful women. Whenever I see one, I never think she's real. The eyes—blue or hazel or green or gold—the way they look, right deep down into a man's libido—the way their hair shines, the way they walk, even the way they stand. . . . " He leaned his forehead on a clenched hand and shut his eyes as if they were dazzled in a glare. "If only they'd realize that all we want them to do is look beautiful . . . that's their genius. It covers some hellish drawbacks, because they're all bitches at heart.

Those that've got hearts." He opened his eyes and stared at Bishop through a frown.

But he was staring at a remembered visual impression that faded out against the wall. Bishop had gone.

He swung round in his chair. It was a half-second before his pupils adjusted their accommodation to take in the room. Bishop was moving past the edge of the dance floor. Beyond the blue spotlight the table was vacant. There was just the empty glass and the paper flakes in the ash tray.

3rd

MOVE

 THEY REACHED the doors almost together.

"Good evening," said Bishop.

She turned.

"Good evening?"

There was no sign of recognition in her eyes. There was nothing in her eyes at all except the cold intense blue.

"I'm Hugo Bishop. We met last night."

"Of course."

"I wondered if there was anything I could do."

Her regard of him was utterly steady. With a quiet politeness she said:

"Do?"

Behind them the band had stopped playing, the man had stopped singing. Someone's laugh sounded over loudly across the room, caught in the hush. People were leaving the dance floor.

Bishop said: "Yes. I believe he was a friend of yours."

"David?"

"Yes."

She glanced down, just as she had when they had been standing by the wreck, and for a moment said nothing. Bishop was aware of movement. Someone was coming in through the archway of the doors. The white shirt of a waiter made a pale blur beyond her shoulder. Round the tables, talk was louder. When she looked up he was trapped again in the cold, exquisite blue. They might have been standing together in a desert place, worlds away.

"Yes, David was a friend of mine. Do you know him?"

It sounded odd, the present tense.

"No. I didn't know him."

Expression had come into her eyes. She studied him. In a moment she said:

"It's kind of you to want to help. But it's not really like that. No one can do anything, now. But thank you."

The band had started to play again. Bishop was left with no choice but withdrawal, but before he could say good night her soft voice came:

"I'd like to dance. Just this one."

He must have shown slight surprise. She added:

"Or are you with someone?"

"No. The pleasure was just unexpected."

They began moving toward the music. The floor was small, intimate, softly lighted. She turned and they were dancing, easily and without reserve as if they had been here all the evening together, sitting at the table over there inside the invisible walls, dancing here among the moving people and unconscious of them, together in a desert place amid the music of the spheres.

She no longer looked at him. Her eyes were clouded whenever he glanced down. She said nothing, not even one quiet word. So that in a little while he began to understand that she wasn't really with him at all. His first impression, formed by the easy sympathy of their rhythm, had been false.

She was still alone, and yet . . . not lonely.

He thought of Miss Gorringe, the way she had spoken about his "sensitive antennae." He was waving them about now, in an atmosphere as strange as a dream. But in a minute or two a clear, cold fact registered in his mind.

Melody was still alone. But she was not lonely. While he held her, and moved with her to the

37

music, she was dancing with someone else.

It gave him an odd feeling, to dance in the shoes of the dead.

It is not pleasant to realize one is being taken deliberately for another person. There is loss of one's identity. And when the other person is dead, it is more than unpleasant. It is eerie. There is loss of one's life.

She glanced up as he missed a step, purposely.

"I'm sorry."

The ice-blue eyes became conscious of their surroundings. She smiled quickly, excusing him.

The music came from the rostrum with a lush gold beat, leading their feet. Her hand pressed firmly against his. Her head was tilted up to look at him.

"You said you were Hugo somebody. Forgive me, but the band was playing and I—"

"Bishop."

"Hugo Bishop." She looked past his shoulder, but the blue didn't cloud again. "We planned to come here tonight, David and I. For a while I've been sitting at the table he'd booked for us. And now I'm dancing with you, instead of with him." A faint smile came. "It's rather refreshing."

They came past her table. He saw the petals of
paper. A waiter was taking the ash tray to empty
it. She said:

"That sounded callous, but it isn't really. He
would think it amusing. I'm sorry you didn't
know him. We three have a lot in common."

"I find it a slightly macabre relationship."

"You would, of course. You only saw what
was left of him." A chill struck Bishop's nape.
Her voice was so casual. "Please tell me—did
he know much about his death?"

"He had no time."

She puckered her mouth.

"I'm glad. No one deserves torture."

She held herself close to him. There was no
style in her dancing, but a natural intimacy. He
sensed in the warm, vital rhythm of her body that
she was glad to be alive. It was difficult, dancing
with Melody, to talk about death.

"It was courteous of you, not to let me see him.
He would have thanked you for that, because
when he was alive he was quite magnificently
so—you said you never met him?"

"No."

"One of the last of the marvelous brutes, rather
like his car—too powerful to run amok and not
smash up."

"He was driving fast—"

"Yes, I know. He always drove like that. I've thought up an epitaph for him: He made his own thunder—God's wasn't enough."

The smile was still touching her mouth. Bishop said:

"I'm sorry I didn't know him. He sounds quite a person."

"Don't be sorry. It wasn't always a good thing to know David Brain. He had a world of his own. He swung it round and round until the whole thing flew to pieces. Some of us managed to duck."

The music stopped. As they left the floor she said:

"You were surprised when I wanted to dance. Why?"

"I was delighted."

"Thank you—but also surprised."

"I had the impression that you felt like being alone this evening; in fact I hesitated before speaking to you this evening. If you had come here to dance, there must be a host of escorts who would have gladly brought you here. I was a stranger."

They stood beneath the archway. Indoor vines grew upwards, twining through trelliswork a-gainst the pillars. Concealed lamps mimicked moonlight. It shone in her eyes.

"Yes, you were. But in a way you're closer to

me than anyone else in the world. That sounds odd?"

Carefully he said:

"Yes."

She shook her head. The dark hair moved in the moonlight.

"The thing that happened to David was violent. All death is violent, even when it happens peacefully in an old man's sleep, because it smashes a world for someone—and the whole world is never bigger than it is in one man's brain. Put a finger over your eyes and you can blot out half London." She did not look away. There was an honesty and an excitement in her eyes that held him still.

She touched his arm. "When his world got smashed, only you were there. You watched something that's changed my life so completely that I'm in another world, too. Perhaps I'm a little bit scared, it's like going to a new school. You are the link."

She didn't make sense; not real sense. This stuff was symbolical, self-deceptive. Bishop realized that when a woman as clear-minded as Melody Carr resorted to this kind of daydream there was one reason. She wasn't calm about the crash, not callous nor casual. She hadn't come here, to a nightclub, within twenty-four hours of a violent death because she felt like going gay. She had come here to be morbid.

He went right to the core.

"Inside," he said, "you're desolate. Aren't you?"

She watched him for a second . . . two seconds . . . three—to be watched by these clear, cold eyes was to feel that time had stopped, and would never start again.

"No," she said at last. "Inside, I'm happy. Singing."

She meant it. Truth was never more naked.

He said: "I can't be expected to understand that. We've met only twice."

"Would you like to see me again?"

"Very much."

"I can find you in the directory?"

"Yes."

"Then I'll phone you some time. Au revoir."

He bowed slightly and watched her go through the arch. Then he went back to his table. Winslow was sitting against the wall, his head tilted on the plush back of the seat, smoke from his cigarette curling past his half-closed eyes. He had been watching the room. Bishop sat down next to him and poured some brandy. Winslow said:

"Of all the people in here who looked as if they didn't want to dance, she was the most. What did you do, put a gun in those glorious ribs?"

Bishop sipped his drink, watching the dance floor.

"It was her idea," he said reflectively.

"Well, I am damned," Winslow said slowly.

"So was I."

"Tell all. I saw no flames, no brimstone, when the what's-it force met the how-d'you-do object."

"No, it was internal combustion."

"Speak on."

"There's nothing to report."

"Don't be such a cagey old son of a clam. You two were babbling the whole time. I was trying to lip-read, but you couldn't have been saying the things I thought you were saying, not even to melody Carr, not even you. If you don't tell me every word that passed between you, I'll finish this bottle on my own and get so sloshed that you'll have to lay on a team of pink elephants to drag me home."

Bishop took pity. He liked Winslow. Winslow had brought him in here. He had met Melody Carr, and that had been the evening's objective.

"Come home with me now, Teddy, and I'll break out some eggs and bacon and black coffee. Then if you want to make a night of it you can just fall down in your tracks and we'll throw a rug over you. Yes?"

Winslow nodded.

"Yes. That'd be nice."

They had one more drink and left. Outside in Park Lane it was moonlight, the real thing. The gunmetal grey Delage had gone. Bishop had a thought: if he wanted to find her again, Gorry would have to start from the beginning, just as she had started earlier tonight; and it might not be so easy next time.

Bishop was not worried. Melody would telephone, tomorrow, the day after, the day after that. Some time she'd ring him. Because he was the link.

4ᵗʰ
MOVE

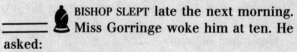 BISHOP SLEPT late the next morning. Miss Gorringe woke him at ten. He asked:

"Where's Teddy?"

She threw back the curtains, dazzling him.

"He went home," she said.

"When?" He squeezed his face, trying to make it work again.

"Just before dawn."

"I don't remember." There was a concrete mixer grinding grit inside the top of his head.

"That doesn't surprise me."

She gave him a cup of scalding coffee and leaned on the windowsill. She added: "It was really rather touching. When I finally managed to get a taxi here, you and Teddy were on the pavement. He had that deep-sea diver's helmet over his head and you were prodding at it with a stethoscope calling out, 'For God's sake answer me, Carstairs, there's a shoal of shark off our port bow!'"

Bishop squinted at her.

"I wish," he said sepulchrally, "you'd stand somewhere else. You're surrounded with bright daylight, and I'm lost without my dark glasses."

She did not move. She said:

"I'm not complaining about the geraniums. I've put them all back in the helmet. But I'm worried about the stethoscope. Hugo, where did you get it?"

He sipped his coffee.

"I don't remember."

"Well, I've been waiting for a doctor to call."

"You mustn't fuss, I don't feel that groggy."

"To call for his stethoscope."

"Oh." He closed his eyes. She moved from the windowsill.

"There's been a phone message from a coroner."

He opened his eyes and squinted at her.

"When?"

"An hour ago."

"Who did we kill—the taxi driver?"

"No, I believe he got off with a crumpled horn.

46

You realize you're wanted at the inquest on David Arthur Brain, next Saturday morning at eleven o'clock. You were the sole eyewitness of the crash."

He mumbled "Yes."

"The coroner rang up to ask if you wanted to go down to Surrey and look over the scene in daylight, to refresh your memory."

He eased himself higher against the pillows. He felt better. The concrete mixer was only grinding grass, now, very quietly.

"When are they shifting the car?" he asked, focusing his eyes on her face.

"This afternoon."

"Well, I'd better get down there. Coming with me?"

"Do you want me to?"

"Yes. You can drive. One of my heads fell off in the night and I don't feel myself without it."

Miss Gorringe took away his coffeecup.

"We'll start immediately after lunch," she said.

"Immediately after yours, not mine. I'll settle for two Alka-Seltzers and a glass of milk."

She turned in the doorway.

"I've seen you recover before. Within half an hour you'll be out of the bathroom and roaring for roast beef." She looked at her watch. "Lunch will be punctually at one o'clock."

She closed the door after her.

He lay back trying not to think about roast beef.

Knoll Hill looked too beautiful to form a background for sudden death. The trees were in full leaf and birds called clear and piping on the summer air. From the curving road there was only a sign of the tragedy: the gap in the black-and-white board fence.

Bishop spent ten minutes looking at the wrecked car. Crawling about among the undergrowth he inspected the chassis. The hydraulic pipe lines to the brake assemblies were unbroken, for they had been protected by the chassis members; there was no leak of fluid except from the cap of the reservoir, and that was due to the angle.

Damage to the steering was heavy: the end of the track rod hung down, with a sheared ball-joint pin, and the drag link was out of line. But this had been caused by the pitching plunge of the car through the trees and its final impact; it was not mechanical failure.

Men came down from the road as he sat on his haunches smoking his meerschaum.

"Going to pull her up?" he asked the foreman.

"Yes, sir." He gazed up the slope. "Take some doin', too."

"Take longer to get 'er up," another man said, "than it took for 'er to come down."

They looked at Bishop, not knowing who he was or whether he had been here before. They were not the night shift who had turned out on Sunday night.

He said: "I've been looking for signs of failure."

A blackbird piped up, right above their heads, mimicking some other call that Bishop couldn't recognize.

The foreman shook his head.

"You're too late, sir. Those signs've gone. It was the human element, I reckon. Nothing wrong with the car—nothing that happened before the crash, like. I've been over it myself an' signed a report." He gazed hopefully at the man with the white pipe. "You know he killed 'imself, I suppose?"

"Yes." Bishop straightened up. The foreman nodded slowly. Pity, it would have been a nice, gruesome story; but the gent seemed to know all about it.

Bishop glanced at him again on a thought.

"You mean it was his fault, the accident?" he said.

"Ay."

Bishop nodded, and left them, going up the slope. He had wondered for a moment if the man had been talking about suicide.

Miss Gorringe was perched on the running board of the vintage Rolls-Royce.

"Through?" she asked.

"Down there, yes." He relit his pipe, leaning on the fender of the car and gazing down the hill. Some seventy-five yards distant, a smaller road forked off and curved away after a short straight, vanishing behind trees.

He wandered down the hill to the fork and stood there for a few minutes. When he looked up Knoll Hill he could see his car, with Miss Gorringe waiting patiently on the running board. The smaller road was signposted to East Knoll.

He came slowly back to the gap in the fence.

"We should have brought a picnic," he said. "All this sunshine and bird song."

"You had an enormous lunch."

He stared vaguely down to the fork in the road again.

"I don't mean I'm hungry. Be an excuse to go *al fresco,* that's all."

"So you're in a romantic mood."

He could just make out the wording on the little signpost. East Knoll.

"M'm?"

"Your mood. Ro-man-tic."

"I mean just a *brioche* and some Bel Paese. And

a bottle of rough red wine."

Patiently she said: "This side of Harrods you won't get *brioches* or Bel Paisa. But we might track down some fish-and-chips in Brixton. We could eat them sitting outside the prison."

He shook his head seriously. "It wouldn't be the same thing, Gorry." When he mooched gently round the car and climbed aboard she called in through the open window:

"Are we going, or are you composing verse?"

After a minute she heard him ask:

"M'm?"

"Oh, for Pete's sake!" She opened the near-side door and climbed in beside him. "In case you're still alive, Hugo, don't reverse by mistake when you start off. The wrecker is parked right behind us."

"Oh." He peered into the mirror. "They'll have their work cut out, you know. Have to use rollers. The wheels won't stand it."

He started the engine. Miss Gorringe said:

"Did you learn anything?"

"Not much."

The grey limousine turned across the road, just as the other car had—the Delage. When he had driven about a mile he stopped and reversed into a farm gateway.

"Tired of going forwards?" said Miss Gorringe.

51

He turned the car back to Knoll Hill. His voice came quietly above the silk-spinning engine.

"Have you ever been to East Knoll?"

"I don't believe so. Is that where we're going now?"

"Yes."

The limousine reached the hill, went whispering through the curve of trees and passed the gap in the fence where the wrecker was at work. A little way on, it slipped quietly into the right fork, and Miss Gorringe saw the signpost.

"So you know the way," she said.

He stared broodingly through the windshield.

"I think I'm just beginning to, yes."

5th
MOVE

A FLY was bumping against the window pane, its thin drone broken by each bump. It sounded like an electric shaver with bad contacts. The top half of the window was open. Outside there was a huge chestnut tree that cast shade over the building, but from the southwest there came sunlight slanting through a window on that wall. It lit the inkwells, and balding heads, the three pips on the police surgeon's left shoulder, a juryman's watch.

Motes of dust drifted through the sunbeam. Above the fireplace a white-faced clock hung on the wall. It said ten minutes past eleven.

"Now I'm going to ask for Doctor Gifford's testimony first, because he has to get back to the hospital as soon as he can."

The coroner looked at the jury. No one objected. The jurymen were sunburned. Three of them had worked half the summer in the fields; their skin was dark leather. Two were shopkeepers; their pale faces looked worried about how the business was getting along without them. One man with spectacles watched the coroner the whole time; two round blobs of reflection from the spectacles were clinging to the wall like a couple of ghostly eggs.

"Doctor Gifford, you made the first full-scale examination of the deceased?"

"Yes, sir."

"Will you please tell us what you discovered to be the cause of his death?"

The jury were intent. They braced themselves for medical mumbo-jumbo, a string of secret, terrible Latin names, words that could kill you in your bed if they appeared on the report-sheet in the sister's hands.

"A fractured skull."

They were disappointed, and relaxed.

"And the cause of the injury, Doctor?"

"Impact of the front of the head against the windshield, the imprint of which was left in the skull."

"Thank you." The coroner looked at the jury.

The jury looked at the coroner. "That is all we need to know, Doctor."

"Right, sir."

The fly buzzed against the window pane. A woman looked round at it. Her chair creaked. The doctor's footsteps were loud as he went past the press table and left the room. The swing door sent a flash of sunlight across all the faces.

Bishop was watching a lean man who sat at the end of the public seats. He was sun-tanned and his suit was made of excellent gabardine, though the cut was American. He was good-looking in a rugged, rather aggressive, way. He had been staring at Melody Carr for five minutes. Bishop had been staring at him for five minutes.

Melody was in black. Her face was pale. A black lace veil reached to her nose; it was not quite short enough to be chic, not long enough to be a habit of grief. But she looked tragic— frail, controlled, and tragic. The coroner had glanced towards her twice, and his bright brown eyes above their pouches were lit with sympathy and something else. It was difficult for a man to look at Melody and think of her solely as a daughter.

Bishop remembered her as she had looked at Romero's. She had been bare-shouldered, sheathed in a peacock-blue miracle by Martineau, the sun still on her skin. Today, nearly a week after that night, she looked desolate.

Inside, you're desolate. Aren't you?

No . . . Inside, I'm happy. Singing.

He had tried to believe that when they had met at the night club she was defying grief. But she had talked about Brain as coolly and as callously as if she had hated him. Underneath the casual phrases and the macabre humor, Bishop had heard a current running, a quiet undertow of exultation. Once, his nape had crawled at the timbre of her voice. It had been easy for him to believe that she told the truth. Inside, she was singing.

This pale face, expressionless with grief held in check, was a sharp contrast. It appeared as sincere as the other expression he had seen in Romero's, when she had smiled slowly. . . . *I've thought up an epitaph for him. . . .*

Bishop decided that there was the choice of three truths. In the night club she had been putting on a magnificent act. Or here in the coroner's court she was doing the same thing. Or there was no act at all: she had exulted in Brain's death the night after it had happened, but now, after six days, she had realized that a man she had known was dead by violence, and she had grown cold with the thought of it.

56

" . . . is a well-known danger to motorists, even in ordinary conditions."

Bishop looked at the coroner and began listening to what he was telling the jury.

"Since the beginning of this year, there have been two serious accidents on Knoll Hill in broad daylight. You have heard the circumstances in which the deceased met his death, so far as the condition of the road is concerned, but we have an actual eyewitness to the accident."

The coroner turned to his sergeant. The sergeant called Hugo Ripton Bishop.

He took the oath in the stand.

"Will you please tell us what you saw of this tragedy?"

As Bishop began, Miss Gorringe heard the blowfly reach the open half of the window behind her, and escape. The buzz died away like a note fading from a plucked cello-string.

She looked at the ash-blonde who sat across the courtroom to her left. She was in black. Her grief appeared to be as deep as Melody Carr's. For minutes now, Miss Gorringe had been amusing herself by trying to judge the difference in the two faces, in their expression. At first glance they were both distressed, were both mourners here. The difference in their despair, Miss Gorringe decided at last, was in the eyes. Neither woman was near tears, but there was a quiet pain in the eyes of the ash-blonde that was not in Melody's. Perhaps there was no room for it. When Hugo had been asked what there had been in Melody's eyes, on the night of the smash, he had said "Sex." He hadn't thought there was room for anything else.

The little ash-blonde was a woman, too, and lovelier in her way than Melody; but her libido didn't shine behind her eyes. They were soft, and grey-green, and there was pain in them.

" . . . So that if you had not pulled your car in towards the side of the road, a head-on collision might have occurred?"

"Would certainly have occurred, sir."

Paper scuffed in the silence. The jurymen were looking at their duplicated plans of the scene, drawn up and signed by the police sergeant who had arrived there first.

The voice of the coroner was hoarse and melodious; he seemed about to clear his throat at any minute, but never did.

"You were fortunate, Mr. Bishop. And quick-thinking, I've no doubt. Now please tell us what happened after the car passed your own, grazing your rear fender."

Miss Gorringe looked down at her map. It was sketched on a sheet of soft quarto paper.

She thought: if the dotted line marked "Ventura" had impinged on the line marked "Rolls-Royce," the rest of the map would be different now, and Hugo wouldn't be here today.

" . . . and ran across to the broken fence," his voice came. She looked up, her large, colorless eyes moving from Bishop to Melody Carr, from her to the ash-blonde, from her to the virile-looking American, from him to the juryman at this end of the bench. He picked at a cuticle.

Without the buzz of the blowfly, the silences in here were profound, whenever a voice ceased. Outside the town hall was summer, drenching the chestnut tree. Green double-decker country buses went past occasionally, and reflected sunlight flickered through the windows of the courtroom and across the ceiling.

"Melody Roberta Carr."

The deceased was a friend of hers?

He was.

How long had she known him?

Some time.

Some time?

Over a year.

Please would she describe what happened between her and the deceased on the night of his death?

"He called at my flat, a little before midnight."

The jurymen were sitting more upright. The one at the end had stopped picking his cuticle and was gazing at the witness with his chin cupped on his hands. The others forgot about their crops, their shops, their loss of valuable time. The sweet, rough voice of the young woman was telling them that the deceased had visited her flat just before midnight. They listened attentively, with the interest of good, honest, masculine, morbid, morally-minded human beings. It was reprehensible that a man should visit this lady's flat only minutes before midnight, in whatever circumstances, but in this suspended moment between all the whys and wherefores of the matter, they envied the deceased. Only a few admitted this, even to themselves. The others were not even conscious that they were guilty of any such emotion. But it was there, in various guises: disapproval, prurience, even disgust at the goings-on of these young London folks. *Mid*night, if you please.

"He seemed to have been drinking."

The coroner glanced up and across his desk.

"Was he actually intoxicated?"

"No. He was just not sober."

"I see."

"I told him I was tired and that I had just got home and wanted to go to bed, but he seemed obstinate about going. I knew him fairly well. He promised to leave soon if I would have a drink with him. We had two whiskies each, but he didn't keep his word."

Miss Gorringe watched the ash-blonde. The ash-blonde was watching the witness. So was the American. The rest of the people were merely looking at her. In the eyes of the blonde and the American there was a steady watchfulness. They would be listening like that, too.

Bishop leaned farther back in his chair. It was a rather fragile, straight-backed chair and it creaked. Miss Gorringe glanced at him. Hugo was hard on chairs, even the massive thing behind his desk in Chelsea.

"After about an hour, I became a little desperate."

She passed a hand over her brow.

The jurymen forgot even to doodle.

The coroner said: "He was a young, powerful man, and self-willed?"

"Yes. He was always difficult to persuade, during the time I knew him. It was less obstinacy than his conviction that in most things he was right." She looked down and for a moment there was silence. Quietly she said: "In most things, he was."

Bishop watched the foreman of the jury. He

was a thin, dark, Welsh-looking man with sparse hair and a pair of long knuckly hands. They rested on the wooden ledge in front of him. He had made notes on his pad. There was no doodling. When the notes were made, the long, angular fingers became perfectly still.

He said suddenly: "What condition was he in, by this time?"

Heads swung. Miss Carr did not look up. The vibrant softness of her voice had begun bespelling the room; now there was opposition. The man's Welsh voice was as soft as hers, and musical. The question had not been rapped out. It had been played in a minor key.

"He was . . . very moody."

She glanced up at the coroner, perhaps sensing that someone in here was against her. The coroner gave the slightest nod of encouragement and looked across to the foreman, who said:

"You mean 'drunk', miss?"

She looked at him directly. Innocence was on his thin, dark face—an expression of innocence that was worse than one of antagonism. He was an implicit man, and she recognized his type and was anxious. She preferred the extroverts.

"No."

The coroner moved his round, wise, robin's head from left to right. The room was no longer stuffy. Ennui was no longer drifting through the window on the balmy summer air. The deceased was no longer just a dead man.

"But he was with you more than an hour," the foreman said. He was standing up. His knuckles rested on the ledge of the bench, with the fingers bent under and out of sight; so that his hands looked like soft, stubby hoofs. "And he was drinking, you say. And he was—'not sober'—when he came." His eyes were full of naïvety. He was only an ordinary man, and did not understand.

"David Brain could drink a great deal without becoming drunk."

They stared at each other.

The coroner looked at Miss Carr.

"You realize how important this is," he said, in his rough, melodious voice, and this time he cleared his throat, but his voice was just the same when he went on: "Apart from Mr. Bishop, you were the last person to see the deceased alive. Your testimony as to his frame of mind and state of body is valuable. We are here to discover as best we can how this man met his death. Now think carefully, please: was he 'very moody' or 'drunk'?"

"He was not drunk."

She closed her eyes wearily, then looked up again.

"His speech was distinct?" asked the coroner gently.

"Yes."

"But he was very moody. How did he show this?"

"One has to know a person to judge their mood. That night, David had made his mind up: he wanted to stay with me until morning."

Everyone avoided everyone else's eyes: the coroner, the witness, the sergeant, the jurymen, the press, the public. Except the Welshman. He was still standing, and he looked straight at Miss Carr. He said—

"Against your wishes, naturally, miss?"

Her head moved.

"Yes."

The coroner looked across his desk, across the faded leather surround of the enormous blotting pad, the two inkwells, the pen rack and the roller rule.

"What happened next?" he asked.

"I decided it was too late to ask anyone's help. People were in bed. I had no friends I could telephone, at least none whose help I could ask without a great amount of embarrassment."

The coroner glanced as if by chance at the foreman of the jury. He sat down, and his long, thin fingers heaped themselves on the wooden ledge like a pile of sticks.

"But we had a mutual friend, down here in the country. His name is Thomas Pollinger and he owns a roadhouse called Beggar's Roost. I decided that the only way I could get rid of David was by suggesting we drove down there and made a night of it."

"I see." The coroner put his hand on the rule and rolled it an inch across the blotting pad. "Did he agree?"

"Yes. He liked the place. We are—we were both members there."

Silence pointed out the slow tick of the clock on the wall behind the coroner's head. He said:

"What was your purpose in making this suggestion?"

"I intended to ask Mr. Pollinger to look after David tactfully, while I drove back home and went to bed. I was very tired." She rested a hand on the edge of the box.

The coroner leaned across to his sergeant. The sergeant nodded quickly and swung a chair from the wall, bringing it round for her.

"Thank you, but I'd rather stand."

The atmosphere tautened another turn.

"Just as you wish, of course." The coroner scratched his chin. "Please go on."

"Both our cars were outside. I said I'd drive him

in mine, but he refused to let me. He was a good driver, and didn't like being driven by anyone. I tried to persuade him. As I have said already, he wasn't an easy man to persuade." The clock ticked three times. "He wanted to drive me in his own car, but I refused."

"Sir?" The foreman of the jury.

"Yes?" asked the coroner.

The foreman looked at the witness.

"Why did you refuse, miss?"

She faced him and said quietly: "I wanted my own car to come home in, after leaving him at the roadhouse."

The coroner asked her: "Were you also afraid to be driven by a man in his condition?"

Her head moved.

"Few people enjoyed being driven by him. He always went very fast."

"I see. What happened, then?"

"He got into his car and I got into mine. We drove off—"

"Did you lead the way, miss?" Her head swung again. "Or did he?"

"He did. He wanted to make a race of it, as the roads were clear at that hour, but I slowed down deliberately, hoping he'd wait for me to catch up."

She looked from the foreman to the coroner,

as if she expected his question next. She seemed on the defensive.

It was the Welshman who spoke.

"And did he wait for you?" His head was tilted to one side.

"No. I lost sight of him for about a mile." She looked down at her hands. "Then I saw the gap in the fence, on the hill, and pulled up."

The foreman asked: "You realized he had crashed through the fence, miss?"

For the first time there was anger in her tone.

"No. I realized nothing of the kind." On the two long tables the reporters were scribbling the whole time now. "I simply realized that it *looked* as if a car had gone through the fence. And I stopped to see if I could help. Motorists do that sort of thing. It's called humanity."

Slowly and gently the coroner said: "We must remember that this is not a criminal trial, but an inquest." He looked along the line of jurymen. "Does anyone want to question the witness further?"

When no one answered, their foreman sat down and stared at his hands. "No, sir," he said for them all.

The coroner nodded to the witness.

"Thank you, that is all."

She walked to the vacant chair against the

wall opposite the jury and sat down, folding her hands.

The coroner added, gazing at his ruler: "It is in the public interest for me to point out that the last witness clearly did her best to help us in this inquiry. It would have been easy for her to have told us that it was the deceased who suggested going to the roadhouse, against her discussion. It would have put her in a much better light, as far as any responsibility is concerned. But she was on oath, and her testimony has been valuable."

He was addressing the foreman of the jury, though he did not glance at him. The foreman watched him steadily.

"Further, the witness faced a very difficult problem, just before the deceased met his death. She was alone in her flat with a young, powerful, self-willed man who refused to leave and who was—in my opinion and in the light of evidence—to some degree intoxicated. Methods of extricating herself from this difficult situation no doubt occurred to her afterwards, but at the time she was slow to consider the risk that the deceased was running in his drive to the road-house; and perhaps that is quite understand-able."

He raised his eyebrows and touched the rule with his fingertips. "Of course, this is not relevant to our purpose here, except in that culpability could be attached to this witness. But I believe that none is admissible."

He turned to the sergeant and spoke quietly. The sergeant passed him a sheet of paper from his own desk.

"The statement from Doctor Gifford refers to there being present in the stomach of the deceased approximately half a pint of alcoholic spirit." He looked up. "Some people would become helplessly intoxicated after drinking to that extent. The deceased was clearly capable in a very high degree, because he could drive a motorcar several miles at a fast pace; and this supports Miss Carr's estimation of his condition: he was much less affected by drinking than is normally found, partly—I suggest—because the habit was of long standing, and partly because he was of strong physique." He looked along the faces of the jurymen. "Whether he would have reached the roadhouse safely if his route had not led him down this dangerous hill, we cannot possibly decide—any more than we can decide whether he would have crashed into the fence even if he had been utterly sober. Similar accidents have happened, in daylight, at this black spot."

He turned to another statement.

"There is the fact of the deceased's being an undischarged bankrupt at the time of his death; but there is no evidence in Miss Carr's or any other's testimony that he was depressed on that night by money worries, unless it is assumed that they started him drinking. In the evidence of the motorist who witnessed the crash, there is no suggestion that the car was driven off the road deliberately: Mr. Bishop has referred to 'an uncontrolled slide' at what seemed to him to be 'a high speed.' Miss Carr says that the deceased 'always went very fast.' There seems to be no confliction of any evidence."

He leaned back and looked at the foreman of the jury.

"Will you please consider your verdict?"

A man three places from the foreman passed a slip of paper along. Another, sitting directly behind him, leaned forward and murmured something. The foreman sent a glance over the rest of them and got up nimbly.

"Accidental death," he said without preamble. "We would like to add that the condition of the deceased due to his drinking might have played a part in the tragedy." He happened to look at Miss Carr, just for an instant. Then he rested his knuckles again on the ledge in front of him. "And we would like to recommend that something is done to make this hill safer, either by special lighting or by a line of red reflectors, or by strengthening the fence along this particular curve. We think it is a case for very urgent attention."

He sat down.

The coroner said that their recommendation would be passed on to the appropriate authorities. The sergeant looked at the constable. The constable opened the swing doors and bolted them back.

Outside the town hall some dozen cars were parked: Bishop's Rolls-Royce, Melody's grey Delage, a blue Cadillac with white-walled tires, a black police car.

The ash-blonde was getting into a Sunbeam-Talbot. Miss Gorringe went over and spoke to her through the car window while Bishop stood talking to Melody. The man in the hand-tailored suit was with her.

"Oh, Everett—this is Hugo Bishop. Hugo, Everett Struve."

They nodded. Struve's eyes were narrowed against the sunglare but they took in all of Bishop. Bishop said to Melody:

"That was a strain for you. Shall we have a drink?"

She did not look at Struve; but Bishop felt she

was waiting for the American to answer for her. He did.

"We're both going right back to London now."

"Thanks all the same, Hugo." She was getting some keys from her bag. "I've still got your number. You're not going away?"

"I don't plan to."

She smiled coolly.

"Good."

She opened the driving-door of the Delage. Struve looked once at Bishop and got into the Cadillac beside it. As she started her engine, Melody said quietly:

"Hugo . . ."

He bent down to the window.

"I'd like to see you tonight. Is that possible?"

"By all means. I'll pick you up."

"No, don't do that. I'll call round—may I?"

"Fifteen Cheyne Mews."

"I'll find it."

He stood back. The Delage turned into the roadway with a thin Continental whine from its exhaust. The Cadillac followed, yawing against the spongy suspension. Bishop stuck his hands in his pockets. Wherever women like Melody went, they had pilot fish.

The little Sunbeam-Talbot was sliding out between the police car and a tiny roadster. Vera

Gorringe was coming across, cool in a tangerine linen suit.

"Quo vadis?"

"Home," he said. They strolled over to the limousine. "Who were you talking to?"

"Sophie Marsham."

"The pocket-Venus?"

"Yes. You'll like her. She's your type."

They drove away, turning northwest in the wake of the other cars.

"I will like her?" he said.

"Yes. I think you should meet her. She's a model."

"A working model?"

"She was David Brain's fiancée."

His face blanked.

"Really?"

"Truly. When I was digging up all the dirt could—in my fastidious way—about David Brain, came across little Sophie. They'd planned to go abroad together. I don't know when. That's one of the things you should ask her about."

He drove for five minutes in silence. Then:

"Why ask her about anything? The issue's cut-and-dried. Accidental death."

"Accidents often happen when personality is under stress, and often the stress goes on afterwards just as tortuously. Or have you decided we're up a dead end?"

"If I have, you can talk me out of it."

She held the wheel while he filled his meerschaum and lit it. She said: "I'd like to do that. There were interesting things going on at the inquest, without a word being said. It was like watching a dead man come to life. The deceased was still very much part of the picture—very much the central figure; the others were circling round: Melody, the American, Sophie. You've met the American—what's he like?"

"He hasn't got much time to be like anything, except hot in the pants about Melody."

"I notice you've picked up his *patois*. What's their relationship?"

"Not vegetable, not mineral."

"The relationship between the—what's his name?"

"Everett Struve."

"Between Struve and Sophie is more intellectual. They were both fighting for the same cause—to pull the other charming couple out of their deadly embrace."

"Because Struve wanted Melody to himself—"

"And Sophie wanted her man back while there was still breath in his body."

Bishop said: "Pity she left things too late."

"Yes." She glanced at him. "It's almost as if she knew she had to hurry. Isn't it?"

After a minute he said: "Where do I meet her, Gorry?"

"She's a member of Beggar's Roost, and she's going there tonight. You can eat and drink there as a non-member; it's a kind of club in a pub. You get thrown out at ten-thirty, of course, as far as the ordinary bars are concerned, unless you're a member. If you're a member you gravitate gently through a door marked 'Private' and order another double. And if you follow the right passage and tread softly you can spend the night playing with a roulette wheel. It's really a well-organized establishment."

"Have you been there?"

"No. This is just routine information."

"What time is Sophie going there this evening?"

"For dinner, about seven."

He hummed through his pipe for a while.

"I've got the Lady in Red calling tonight. I don't see how we can fit them both in."

"Melody Carr?"

"Yes. But I don't know what time she's coming. I think she wants to get away from Struve."

"Then telephone her and suggest she calls late. Say, nine-thirty. You can be back from Telbridge by then."

75

"Beggar's Roost is at Telbridge?"

"Yes. Two miles out of the village, towards town."

He said doubtfully: "I don't think I can learn as much from Sophie as I might from Melody. I told her I'd pick her up at her flat, but she said she'd come round to me. I'd like to see her flat. Brain spent the last few hours of his life there; he said his last words there, drank his last drink. Sometimes you can sense the atmosphere in a place—"

"If you ever get near her dressing table, tell me what scent she wears. I think it's *Ashes of Dead Lovers*."

"And what about little Sophie?"

"She wears *Frustration*."

"She didn't look very frustrated."

"She's not the type to show what she is. That's one of the things you'll like about her. But you may be right. She might have got rid of her frustration now that the engagement's broken off. But see her; I've a feeling."

"All right, I'll put five bob on."

They reached Cheyne Mews and lunched on salad. Halfway through the afternoon Miss Gorringe came into Bishop's study and found him talking to the Princess Chu Yi-Hsin. They were both on the floor, Bishop at full length and the

Princess on her haunches. Between them were a chessboard and pieces. Every time he stood a piece on a square, she shot out a smoky paw and dabbed it over.

Bishop didn't look up. Quietly he murmured:

"Watch this, Gorry."

He stood up a red Pawn; the Siamese sent it flying. He tried a Knight, a Rook, a Bishop and a King. The paw hooked them down with a rattle; the limpid blue eyes blinked slowly, satisfied.

"But she always does that," said Miss Gorringe.

"No, look." He stood up the white Queen. The cat just sat and looked at it. Bishop raised his head.

"Every time, Gorry."

"She won't knock down the Queen?"

"Just won't touch it." He looked at the Siamese. It wasn't important, but somewhere inside that small, sleek head, somewhere deep in the primitive cat's-brain there was something that wouldn't let it dab out at a Queen. The shape of the piece was different from that of the others, but similar to the King's. Yet the Kings went spinning as soon as he stood them up: never the Queens.

Miss Gorringe shivered. Mysterious selectivity in animals was sometimes uncanny to watch; and cats were full of it.

77

Gently Bishop put out a finger, and knocked down the Queen. The cat lifted its head and looked at him between the eyes; that was all. But for an instant he felt as Gorry did. Their brains were immeasurably superior to this animal's, but the cat knew the answer to something, and they did not.

"You busy?" he said.

"No."

"I've been trying to work out situations. Like to help?"

"If I can."

"Well, you'll have to start by removing this electronic brain. She'll knock the pieces down, all except two." He looked at the Princess Chu Yi-Hsin. "Shove off, you uncanny Kilkenny."

The Siamese stared at him for a moment and then got up from its haunches, mincing away towards the davenport, disdain incarnate.

Bishop picked up the red King and stood it in the center of the checkerboard.

"David Arthur Brain, drunkard, bankrupt, dangerous driver, deceased. The central figure—as you say, Gorry—round which the others turn."

From the davenport the cat watched, pretending not to. Not for all its cat's-world would it admit to further interest in the ivories; but it watched, slyly and sideways, flexing a delicate whisker against a cushion.

"Beside him, Melody." The red Queen stood next to the King, facing him in the center of the board. "I feel they should share the honors."

He placed a white Knight obliquely from the King and checking him. "Everett Struve, who didn't necessarily wish Brain any harm, provided he kicked the illustrious bucket and left a clear field surrounding Melody."

"Oddly enough," said Miss Gorringe, "Struve didn't seem very top-o'-the-world today, although number-one rival came to honorable grief and left exquisite lotus blossom free for anything fancy."

"That is a point. But maybe little poison-orchid don't muchee care for excellent survivor. I don't myself, but I think it's his tailor that puts me off."

He stood the white Queen to balance the white Knight.

"Sophie Marsham was a protagonist of Struve's. They both eyed Brain with less than deep affection, for their different reasons. But the white Queen is obliquely attacking the red at the same time—"

"Providing it's her move next."

"Providing that. It depends whether the game's over. With the red King nibbling gently at the dust, it seems like checkmate. But these other little angels might not worry about the rules."

"A tournament of attrition."

"Yes. Until there's one last pawn left on the board, to die of old age."

He toyed with a white Bishop, looking reflectively at the squares. "White, because as yet I'm innocent of any skulduggery in this particular schemozzle—"

"Give yourself time," said Miss Gorringe.

He put the white Bishop beside the white Queen.

"Next to our Sophie, since you suggest I'm liable to become sweet on her—"

"Repulsive expression—"

"But delightful sensation. And under attack from the white Knight, since I have a rough idea that Everett doesn't like me very much."

"Why not? If one has to resort to logic and not his instinct."

"I'm deeply offended. However, as far as logic goes, Struve didn't like the way Melody talked secret things in my ear while he was starting fires in all those countless cylinders of his, outside the coroner's court. He suspects my humble pants are incandescent about Little Poison Ivy, same like his."

He leaned back on his elbow. Ash fell from his

pipe, scattering over a corner of the checker-board.

"Thing I'd like to know," he said, "is why Melody seems to have hated Brain. I told you some of the things she said at Romero's. Even if she'd been trying to put a bold face on a broken heart, she couldn't have said things like that without a certain amount of morbid pleasure; and it came through in her voice."

"It was sincere."

"Yes."

After a while Miss Gorringe said: "Did you think she was telling the truth, at the inquest?"

"I thought she was twisting it."

"I don't blame her. The little Welshman was being very tough."

"He wanted to see her squirm."

She looked at him in surprise.

"Why?"

"Because when a man has an itch for a woman whose sex-magnetism goes through solid walls, the next best thing to taking her is to have power over her—"

"Aren't you putting too much on a sexual basis, Hugo?"

"I'm putting *everything* on that basis, where Melody is concerned. She's a symbol for it— blatant, patent and flagrant. She's a woman with trouble round her, and there's been a violent death. Looking at Melody, it'd be absurd to go poking about for motives other than lust, jealousy, frustration and hate among the people who have anything to do with her. Remember what Teddy Winslow told you? Meeting Melody would be like walking into a fire."

He got up, and stood looking down at the pieces on the chessboard. His feet were astride and his arms were folded, his pipe cupped in one hand.

"And Brain got burned," he said.

6th

MOVE

BEGGAR'S ROOST was a long, low shack of a place, part coachhouse, part barn, part farmhouse, but Pollinger had supervised its conversion, and it was good. He had spent nine thousand, laying new parquet floors, new paths in the grounds, a gravel drive between thick laurels; putting in a plumbing system that fed four bathrooms, ten bedrooms, two kitchens, three bars and the fountain in the sun loggia above the lily pool; knocking down walls, fitting up doors, straightening out corners, making the whole place water-proof, draft-proof, weather-proof, and worry-proof. Nine thousand, and Pollinger was still paying off.

He was a small man. His shoulders seemed to stick out in front of him and he hurried after them wherever they went. They went into some odd places. Pollinger never backed out of anywhere. If he came upon trouble he just went on and broke through the opposite wall, and by the time you had counted the bricks he was gone. He was not a gentle man, but he was a gentleman; and so far as people knew, he was honest. Some people do not know very far: these were his friends.

Bishop had most of this from Miss Gorringe; the rest he sized up for himself.

"Yes," Pollinger said, "that was bad."

They were talking about a member. Brain.

Pollinger looked at his heavy gold signet ring, turning it in the dying red of the sunset and watching it flash.

"Did you know him?" he asked. His small, naked-pated head jerked up.

"No. I understand I missed something."

"Yep. A man, was he. Built like a bull, but for speed too, you know? And young. Only thirty-five or so. Too young to die. Too full of good, hot blood. We were sorry, all of us." He looked away, his forehead a mass of wrinkles. "I mean my gang—the members here. I'm fond of them. They were fond of him."

He shook his head as if there were just no more to be said.

When he seemed to have got over his moment of curiously aggressive grief, Bishop said:

"I believe Miss Marsham's coming here for dinner. I was hoping to meet her."

"Yes?"

"We were both at the inquest, but I felt she just wanted to get away, afterwards. I left it till now."

Pollinger frowned at Bishop's suit, put it at fifty guineas plus and decided to show him round the Roost. Membership wasn't full. People had to have money to come here. These days, people with money were a species of Dodo, and Pollinger had a Dodo-shaped net. He had made it himself. It was a fancy design; it was designed for people's fancies: the ones that weren't easily satisfied in an austere world on the edge of a radio-active volcano.

You wanted to get gay at four in the morning in an atmosphere of bucolic old-worldliness? Dance on the rose-lawn in the moonlight to the tune of gypsy violins? Drink absinthe, poteen, Vodka, Imperial Tokay out of goblets or shepherds' gourds? Sit with a magnum and dote cosily on the cabaret of nubile mobile nudes? *Faites vos jeux?*

Pollinger could give you these simple pleasures. They were costly, but then you were a Dodo. Or you wouldn't be here.

"She has a table booked," he said. He gave Bishop a drink at the Alpine Bar and looked at his watch and said: "I'll show you round. Have you time?"

"I'll make it."

The only three things that were not on view were the cabaret, the casino, and the absinthe. Everything else was legal. Bishop had only Miss Gorringe's word for the fact that if the police made a raid on this place, half the membership would land in court, and Pollinger in jail.

Pollinger didn't worry about raids. He was selective in his clientele. They were people who didn't like publicity. They just wanted fun, and they had the price. One day, maybe, someone would start talking to the good-looking young college boy at the American Bar in some other place, and the subject of gambling would come up, and they'd ask him if he ever looked in at Beggar's Roost for a spell at the wheel. And the good-looking young college boy would be Someone at the Yard.

But Pollinger didn't worry. One day, it would happen. People were human. They talked a lot without their lawyers. But it was like worrying about getting run over tomorrow, or breaking your neck down the stairs. It could happen. Anything could.

Besides, the Roost was respectable. There was no little projection room here, with films from Paris; no marihuana; no private suite of rooms. The cabaret girls worked hard for good pay. You could watch them. You couldn't buy one. If you wanted things like that you had to go to Leicester Square. This was a country club.

"There can't be another place like this," Bishop said, "in the British Isles."

"Might be a few north," Pollinger said, "where the industry is." He was a practical man. "Down south there's not enough money. This kind of place is very expensive, for you and for me. Got our own mushrooms growing here—we buy spawn. Conservatories full of orchids. Trap our own rain water, worked out the system myself. Women come here for their complexion's sake. Thirty-four pounds a year for ice, just ice in the drinks—I've been assessing costs this quarter. Money melts."

He grinned suddenly as if he had been telling a funny story. "But good grief! We're happy most of the time." He nodded to Bishop and left him without another word.

Sophie came at a quarter to seven, alone. She was signing in when Bishop said hello.

"Your aunt said you might show up here," she said. "I was talking to her outside the courtroom."

87

They shook hands. She didn't smile. She looked lost.

"Would you like an aperitif?"

"Thanks, I would.' "

She passed a long mirror as they walked into the Loggia Bar. It framed her nicely for a moment. She was in a black cocktail tunic with a motif of silver brocade; the skirt flared as she turned—

"I've been worrying, all the afternoon. I felt I should have given evidence at the inquest."

There was no faltering in her speech. The inquest might have been on anyone at all, a stranger. But there was no trace of the quiet exultation that had sounded in Melody's voice. This one was clear and bleak and calm, like a record on a machine.

"Evidence of what?" said Bishop. He ordered Dubonnet.

"Well, there was nothing substantial, I suppose. I expect that's why I just sat there." Without the slightest change in her tone—"Are you a friend of Melody Carr's?"

"We've met once, socially?"

"Did you know her before the accident?"

"No."

They sipped their drinks. She said:

"And David. You didn't know him?"

"No."

He was getting away with monosyllables. He had expected to have to talk his way carefully through a lot of non-essentials before he could ask her what he wanted to know; but she was leading. She wanted to know something, too. He wondered what.

"Have we met before?" She looked at him very directly. She had grey-green eyes. "I've a feeling I know you."

"This is the first time. But I hope it isn't too late."

She turned her head and watched the fountain. It had a single plume of water that curled over and splashed down over green marble. Fern fronds dipped and trembled as drops fell on them. He saw her eyes change; the expression went out of them. She wasn't watching the fountain anymore, but was thinking about something a long way from here; someone, perhaps; possibly Brain.

Bishop said nothing. He wanted to study her. She had a quaint, sharply-chiseled little profile with a child's nose and high cheekbones. Her mouth was quiet; there was obstinacy in the small pointed chin. The bright floss of her hair looked metallic against the black Medici collar, but it was natural.

She seemed too small, in many ways too delicate, to have partnered a man like Brain; but there was no fragility in her features; in miniature, they were strong.

"You were nearly killed, weren't you?"

She was glancing at him suddenly and he was caught.

"No, I wouldn't say that—"

"But another yard in your direction . . . according to the little map we were given."

He shrugged.

"These days, we live by inches . . . according to the statistics."

"You believe it was really an accident?"

He looked into his glass.

"The evidence I gave was absolutely true."

"Yes, of course." After a moment she said slowly, "You know we were going to be married, in Paris?"

"I think I heard that—"

"Did Melody tell you?"

The question had been quick. He said: "No."

Slowly again she said: "He promised to be on the Golden Arrow with me, the next day." Her mouth hardened. "Just one of those things."

"I can't help admiring your philosophy. The shock must have been paralyzing."

"In a way. In a way, it was also a relief."

He wrenched his mind round to a new focus. Melody had been "singing, inside." She had not been in love with Brain; Melody had never been in love with anyone; in her world there was no room for two; nor had there been in Brain's. But this girl had been going to marry him ... and his death was a relief.

"You mean," he murmured carefully, "you expected him to smash himself up, sooner or later?"

"Not quite that." She was staring at the vines that climbed trellis wires along the walls. Whatever she looked at, she didn't see. "Being with David was like being caught up in a magnificent machine, or being driven very fast in a powerful car. You enjoyed it, and a lot of the time there was ecstasy, the kind you feel at high speed when you know you're going well above the safety limit. But sometimes you wished you could pull up, and feel the firm ground and listen to silence."

Her voice trailed off. The fountain splashed with fragile musical insistency like an eldritch orchestra forever tuning up. Bishop thought: two very attractive women, both glad he was dead. How many more were there? Brain had known more than two. And how many men, burning for Melody, men like Struve? How many people were glad he was dead?

Some of them were here, at Beggar's Roost.

Too young to die. We were sorry, all of us. I mean my gang—the members here. I'm fond of them. They were fond of him.

But two of them were glad. Struve made a third. Who else?

Bishop began feeling sorry for Brain. He seemed to have had a lot of friends; but so many had the death wish in them. It could be that Bishop was about the only person in the world feeling sorry for him. He realized that if he had known the man, as these others had known him, the pity would probably go; not even begin.

He suddenly wanted to know more about David Arthur Brain who'd made his own thunder because God's wasn't enough. A man couldn't help how he was built, the way he ticked. This fierce blaze had been quenched early: Brain was thirty-five. Perhaps he hadn't quite found himself, or what he had really wanted, because he'd gone too fast.

Bishop wasn't quick to sympathize with a man who got drunk and then went wild with his car. The grey Rolls-Royce had nearly been wrecked too. Sophie was right: another yard, and the death rate might have been doubled on Knoll Hill that night. Brain might have killed some-

one else—anyone walking on the roads, even
a tramp. That drive in the Ventura had been
murderous; it was just that there weren't any
victims about.

But there was Brain's point of view. He had
taken his last drink, got into his car for the last
time—thirty-five years of what? When had his
death begun? When the wheels had gone into
their slide over the wet roadway, or a year ago
when he had met Melody? Or before that, long
before that, when he was a kid?

Dead now. Who was sorry? Anyone at all?

"That must have sounded inhuman," her light
voice said.

"To say it's a relief?"

She nodded.

He finished his drink.

"It sounded honest. Did you really believe he'd
be on the Golden Arrow with you, the next morning?"

She said: "It wouldn't surprise you if I said that
I didn't. But it wouldn't be true. I—was here,
that night. I didn't know where David was, until
Melody rang up. I was talking to Tom Pollinger,
and he took the call. He said she and David
were driving down, from her flat. I'd believed
his promises, until that moment. But when Tom
put the telephone down, it was like watching the

boat train pull out, without us—"

"He'd promised not to see her again?"

"How did you know?"

"You mentioned 'promises.' That seems a likely one."

She said nothing, for minutes. He pressed the bell push on the wall. The waiter had come and gone with the order before they spoke again.

He said: "You asked me if I thought it was an accident, a little while ago. Why?"

She thought for a moment, then shivered suddenly.

"I don't know. Let's not talk about him anymore."

Lightly he said: "Let's not." He offered her a cigarette but she shook her head.

"I don't smoke." He put the case away. "But you may."

"I smoke a pipe. I keep these for my friends." As the waiter brought their drinks he asked: "Are you going back to town tonight?"

"I'm not sure. I feel a bit lost. Are you?"

"Yes, I'm not a member."

"Would you like me to introduce you?"

"Thanks, perhaps. I like Pollinger—he showed me around the place just before you came."

"All of it?"

"I imagine so."

She sipped her drink. "You're having a meal here, before you go back?"

"Yes."

"Share my table."

"May I?"

"I don't want to eat alone. I've friends here, but they'll be a fraction scared of me tonight. Inquests on dead lovers lead to tears. That paints them in bad colors: I mean they won't want to disturb me if they see me alone."

For the first time she smiled. "And anyway I'd like to go on talking to you. You give me the feeling that nothing I said would be taken wrongly, and that's a good feeling."

"Rather like talking to oneself."

"No, to a friend. I haven't talked to anyone about David since it happened. I don't know what started me tonight. But now I've said it all, or most of it, I feel better." She clasped the Dubonnet in her cupped hands and said without looking at him, "Do people get things off their chest to you, when you don't even know them?"

"Sometimes."

"And do you mind?"

"I like it."

"You're curious?"

"Interested."

"What do you do?"

"To live?"

"Yes."

"Eat. I find it a prerequisite."

"I'm sorry. Let's go in—"

"That wasn't a parry. It's just that it'd take a long time to explain what I do for a living."

She stood up. He took her glass and put it down for her. She said: "The food here is good."

"And you've an appetite?"

She met his eyes directly and in a moment said with a faint smile: "Let me be honest again. Yes."

They said nothing more about the crash or the inquest or Brain, during the meal. She gave no lead in that direction, as she had done earlier; and he was left wondering what it was that she had wanted to know from him. There had been only one question that had made him think. She had asked: "Do you really believe it was an accident?"

The one in his mind was the same. Did she?

7th

MOVE

♗ MISS GORRINGE was out when Bishop reached Cheyne Mews. It was past nine-thirty and he knew Melody had arrived. The grey Delage was outside.

She was sitting behind his desk, in the study. The Princess Chu Yi-Hsin was on her lap. He thought they made a nice picture. Behind Melody the last of the sunlight sent a dusty, orange glow against the windows; there was no lamp burning in the room. They were both very still, the woman and the cat.

He closed the door.

"Hello," she said.

"I'm very sorry—have you been here long?"

"A few minutes. Your secretary said make myself at home."

Sometimes his aunt, sometimes his secretary. Gorry rang the changes, according to what role she felt it best to adopt with different people. It should have led to confusion, but it seldom did. The last time was when she had answered the door with an armful of empty bottles. She dropped all her aitches and said she was the char. The caller saw her again the same evening, dining with Bishop at the Casa Maria.

"I'm glad. Will you have a drink?"

"Not now." Her long sun-brown hand caressed the cat's ear. From half-way across the long room, Bishop could hear it purring. He said:

"I've never seen that happen before."

"What happen?"

He sat one haunch on the edge of the desk.

"She's never let anyone take liberties unless she's known them at least three months."

"We're on the same wave length. I can feel the electricity."

She looked up at him. She had a cat's quiet, and cat's eyes. Bishop didn't respond to this intense animal gaze, because he wouldn't let himself. He didn't want this woman. But he knew how easy it must be for a man to plunge suddenly to the very depths of wanting her, faced with the light icy blue that never wavered. In its frankness alone she was wholly naked.

Even in the dusty courtroom, where they had all been gathered to decide how a man had died, Bishop had seen what had happened to the wiry little Welshman. All the questions he had put were reasonable; but it was the impulse and antagonism behind them that had been so clear, even to the coroner.

"What are you thinking?" she asked. Her voice was black velvet.

"About you."

"Your face was hard."

The cat jumped, landing on the desk. It sat like a sphinx in the flushed glow of sundown.

"Thoughts don't always show in faces."

"What were you thinking, about me?"

"How dangerous you are."

She leaned her bare arms along the arms of the chair. The light sent their skin gold. She wore no bangle, no earrings, no brooch. Nothing detracted from the sheer simplicity of the black evening sweater, the dark fall of her hair.

"Dangerous?"

"To men."

"To you?"

"No. Men."

"As a conversational generality—"

"As a fact."

"A personal one—"

"But you don't really want an apology."

She smiled. "No. They don't ever talk like this—"

"They?"

"Men. The ones you mean."

"Struve?"

The smile went. "For one."

"He's not a friend of yours. Otherwise I couldn't have said it."

"You don't hedge very much."

"You want me to?"

"No, God forbid. This is new. Go on."

"I think I've finished."

He leaned on one arm, his hand touching the corner of the chessboard, his head tilted to face her.

She said: "I'm sorry you have. And again it's unusual. The others go on interminably."

"They don't talk as I do, you say. How do they?"

"Oh, they say how magnificent I am. They've never met anyone like me. I've changed their lives."

"All true. Especially of Brain."

"That was mutual." Her tone was steady. "He was magnificent. I'd never met anyone like him. He changed my life, too."

The cat closed its eyes against the sun's glow.

Its shadow was humped on the carpet, bigger than it.

"He said I was dangerous, too." She looked at him steadily. "You're slight and quiet-voiced and calm; almost his opposite; but there's an odd likeness. In the way you think."

"About you?"

"No." She smiled again. "He loved me. He died loving me."

"Faithful to the last."

For seconds she sat without answering, just watching him. At last she said: "Opposites again. You think of me as poison. Don't you?"

"No. Only when you're taken."

"The word has so many meanings—"

"Down from the shelf."

She laughed, lifting her head suddenly. It was a free, soft-throated laugh. The Siamese opened its eyes and stared.

"My God, Hugo, you feint fast—"

"I have to."

"The others were so slow. All they could think about was their libido. It got them clogged up. They couldn't get past it—"

"Twice you've said 'the others.' As if I were in a group."

"You are. Of men."

"You hate half the world. The male half."

As though she had only now realized it she said:

"Yes, that's true."

"But why? Isn't it at your feet?"

"Should that make me like it?"

"Your point."

He got off the desk and began walking about. She watched him. In the room the sunlight was deepening. She was hardly more than a dark silhouette in the great carved chair. Behind her the windows were Venetian-red.

"I hated them from a long time ago."

Her voice scarcely carried to him.

"Another thing is that something seems to have come to an end." He spoke lightly. " 'The others *were*' ... 'I *hated* them' ... "

"My words are under close scrutiny, Hugo."

"They're interesting. Words shouldn't just be said and lost." He stopped pacing and stood near the desk, looking down at her. "But why this past tense?"

"I hadn't realized I was speaking in the past."

"I wonder if it's because Brain was the last of 'the others.' "

She stood up. Her body was long and lithe as she moved towards him, hands loose behind her. He knew she must have looked like this to many men, moving near them while they watched with their breath tight in their throats.

He knew how they had felt; there was blood in him too. It was hard not to forget suddenly that she had a mind as well as this maddening body, these naked blue eyes. Her mind was alert; he mustn't turn his back on it; she'd be as quiet as a cat before she pounced.

"You're very interested in David," she said.

She stood so near him that he felt her warmth. Her face was tilted to look at him. Her eyes were wide and she did not blink. They were hideously beautiful.

"Yes," he said.

Softly she asked: "Why?"

To look into these eyes was to be lost in something. Even thought was an effort.

"I've heard so much about him from other people."

"From me. Who else?"

No bangle, nor earring, nor brooch. Just the honey-gold skin, the flaring ice of the irises, the dark tide of hair. Not beautiful. Beauty was innocent.

"People who knew him."

"Who?"

"His friends."

Anger came into her voice, soft though it was.

"When did they tell you?"

"Since he died."

"What did they tell you?"

"How he lived."

She moved and her body touched him.

"Hugo."

"Yes?"

"Your face is hard again."

"I'm looking at something dangerous."

"You're thinking with your head."

"I use it for that."

The crimson of her mouth was parted.

He began thinking of her. Forgetting she had a mind.

"Suppose we hadn't talked—didn't know anything about each other," she said on her breath.

"Well?"

"Your voice is hard too."

"Suppose we hadn't talked. Well?"

"And I came to you like this."

"Suppose that."

"What would you have done, then?"

"It's too late to matter."

Her warmth was intense. The room was silent.

"Are you sure?"

Again it was like being alone with her in a desert place, and out of touch. All life was trapped in this one fierce animal body.

"Yes," he said.

She shivered.

"Cold?" he asked gently.

She stood away from him.

"Yes. I came too near. How long have you been dead?"

He laughed. It was partly relief. He said:

"Let's have a drink."

She was smiling. "You're genuinely amused, aren't you?"

"Aren't you?"

"I suppose I am. Perhaps more stimulated than amused. Have you Scotch?"

"And soda?"

"Lovely."

He poured out their drinks, saying: "stimulated—another word for infuriated?"

She was still smiling.

"Even if it were, I couldn't admit it, could I?"

"Oh, I think so. To me. I feel very kindly disposed towards you, Melody."

"Even smug. Triumphant."

"Because I'm obviously one of the very few men who could be as near you as that without getting burnt to a frazzle?"

"The first." She said it with a kind of puzzlement. "The first one who is really a man, I mean. The others couldn't have been burned by anything at all. The fancy boys."

"I'm surprised you mix with such queer company."

She laughed. "Some are hard to tell. It's like pressing the trigger and finding the thing isn't loaded."

He passed her drink.

"But that's what happened with me."

She shook her head. "No. You were fighting like hell. Weren't you?"

"I was."

She released her breath, ran fingers through the dark hair, throwing it back.

"Then at least I can face myself in the glass again."

"Is it that important to you, that only one man could hold out against you, and he had to fight like hell?"

"Yes, Hugo." She tilted her drink. "Three cheers for the winner."

"One and a half each. It was a draw."

They took their drinks over to the windows. There was a deep bay behind the desk, in which the great chair stood. The hot red lozenge of the sun had gone down behind the houses now. The air in the street looked colored, purpled with shadow.

"An odd end game," she said. He followed her glance. On the desk was the chessboard, with the five pieces still as he had left them: two Queens, a Knight, a King, a Bishop. He said:

"Yes, isn't it."

"A problem you've given yourself?"

"Yes. Can you solve it?"

"I don't know chess well enough. It takes a certain type of mind. Generalship. I'm always wary of a chess player, especially one who writes exhaustive theses on human behavior."

He raised his brows. She turned her head, looking across the room. The strong line of her throat was beautiful in the gloom. "*The Anatomy of Guilt,* by H.B. Ripton ... *Man in Crisis,* by H.B. Ripton ... *Primitive Instinct,* by H.B. Ripton. ..."

"My favorite author. An American."

She looked back at him.

"I'd have believed that, because they're all American editions and people fill their bookshelves with their favorite authors. But the coroner's sergeant called Hugo Ripton Bishop this morning. Any further disclaimer will be ignored."

He shrugged. She smiled and said, "For all I know I've just been trying to seduce a professor of psychology. No wonder the going was tough."

"The technique was terrific." He looked out of the window. Street lamps were coming on.

"Did you come here to do just that?" Before she answered he added: "No, you couldn't have. You would have asked me to your flat instead. The atmosphere would have been more conducive than here."

"You work everything out, don't you?"

"On the other hand, someone might have shown up at your place. Struve. Not to be countenanced."

Her warm knuckles touched his. Their glasses were held almost together. She was looking down at them. She said:

"Hugo, battles of wits bore me. I haven't the equipment, especially when I'm up against a master. I'm going to give you best." Faint light from the street shone on her face. In here they had passed from day to night. "I was afraid we'd be disturbed by Everett, yes. He's being slightly importunate. Since he came back from the States two days ago I've had no peace. I—"

"Did he fly?"

She looked up.

"Yes, why?"

"Because he heard about Brain's being killed?"

She was silent for a long time, then said softly:

"You're still at work. You're interested in David, and everything and everyone that had anything to do with his life. I want to make a bargain with you. I don't particularly mind how much you find out about him, and there's no one in this world who can tell you more than I can."

For the first time he heard a note of pure honesty in her voice. "It's something quite new for me to persuade a man to do what I want—especially this. Tomorrow I'm going to the South of France for a few days. I'd like you to come with me. If you will, I'll tell you about David."

"Why are you going?" His tone was polite.

"Partly to get away from Everett. If you come, please don't let anyone know you're with me. He knows your name and might find out where you'd gone. And he'd follow."

Politely again: "Why would he follow?"

Her knuckles began pressing against his. Her voice was edged.

"Fantastic as it will seem to you, Professor, the man wants me."

He smiled in the faint light. She murmured through her teeth: "My anger amuses you."

"It's not quite that. Humor's an odd thing. When someone trips over and goes full-length, most of us feel like laughing. And if he's our best friend, we just bust our sides. Because we know him, and we know just how furious he is. And for some reason that's plain funny. In the last few minutes I've begun to know you, a little. And your frustration is getting funnier, because of that."

He could feel her anger. It was tangible.

"I'm not staying here until you double up."

"I don't expect you to. And anyway, I shan't. After a little time, slapstick palls."

"I don't think I've ever met such an insufferable egotist—"

"Your life is full of new experiences, tonight. Mine is, too."

Her body tensed with surprise as he kissed her mouth. She did not move. Her breath was held. He felt the beat of her heart. Her response was slow, but she put it into French.

In a moment she said:

"You're an exponent of the unexpected."

"But you've expected that, most of your life."

"Never from you. What made you?"

"Pig-headedness. Because you'd stopped trying to make me."

"Not because you wanted to?"

"That goes without saying."

"You're coming to life?"

He shook his head.

"No. But Death takes a holiday, sometimes."

She finished her whisky and looked at him for a minute.

"I'm beginning to hate your guts a little less."

"Now don't get sentimental."

Her laughter was rich.

"I haven't done that for a long time, Hugo."

"Done what?"

"Laughed."

"It sounds nice."

"It feels nice."

"Could be the Scotch."

"No. It's you. Darling, come to Monte with me."

He said: "All right."

Her eyes widened. "Unexpected again. I imagined there'd be obstacles. You're foot-loose?"

"And fancy-free."

She put her tumbler on to the desk and gripped his elbows. Her voice was rough with excitement.

"Tomorrow? By air?"

"In the morning."

She began speaking quickly, without thinking the words out first. They just came honestly. "I don't know why I'm excited, but I am. Maybe because since David got killed I've wanted to get away, maybe because I want to get away from Everett now that he's here. And there's a reason I can't tell you about yet. I'm excited because you're coming with me, just like that, on the crest of a wave. In an insufferable way you've got under my skin and I itch. It's a feeling I've not often had before."

She parted her lips and clenched her white teeth in a quick animal smile. Through them she said: "It's nice."

He picked up her glass and took it with his to the cabinet. Over his shoulder:

"Melody, listen. I think you're dangerous. I think you're poison. I wouldn't trust you an inch. You've got too much body and too little heart and your head's screwed on so much the right way that no man can be with you five minutes with his guard down—and get away with it."

He came slowly back with the drinks. Pale light from the street winked on the tumblers.

"I'm saying this because I don't want you to get any cozy ideas about our trip to Monte Carlo. You said it was a bargain. We're going on those terms. You want me to go with you for your own reasons. I'm going with you for mine."

He held out her drink. She took it. He said:

"This morning there was an inquest. On the evidence, there was no other verdict possible. Accidental death. But it wasn't the smash that killed Brain. Not really. It mangled him up, but he was dead before that. I want to know what killed him, and some time in the next few days when we're lying in the sunshine on the Mediterranean sands I'm going to ask you."

She stood still as a cat. Her eyes were luminous. A tremor passed across the surface of the drink in her hand; then it was smooth again.

His voice was almost gentle.

"Because I think you know."

8th

MOVE

BISHOP SWUNG his foot, staring at the ceiling. He said: "And you were right. I like your little Sophie."

Miss Gorringe poured more coffee for them both.

"I'm glad. Did she tell you much?"

"Not really. The thing that impressed me about her was the fact that she's the second person who feels relieved by Brain's death. I've the feeling there may be others." He glanced down at the clock. "Incidentally, I'm leaving for Monte in three hours. Plane goes at noon."

Miss Gorringe passed his cup of coffee.

"Going alone?" she asked.

"No. I'm going with Melody. She asked me to."

Miss Gorringe looked at him for a couple of

114

seconds with her colorless, negative eyes. Then she said:

"It's bad enough your playing with fire, Hugo, but now you're going to do it so far away that I shan't be able to get a hose on you in emergencies."

"Won't be any emergencies."

She shrugged. "What orders, during your absence?"

"None. Except that if Struve phones to ask where I am, please tell him."

"Simply that you've gone to Monte?"

He nodded, sipping his coffee.

She asked: "Shall I say you've gone there alone?"

"You don't know."

"But he will?"

"That is the idea, yes. Melody asked me to tell nobody where I'd gone; she doesn't want Struve to follow; but I do."

"Why?"

"Because he's liable to be a troublesome person, and when trouble starts, things quicken. I don't plan a cozy swimming-party for two in the next few days. I can find out a lot more from Melody, but if Struve's there it'll raise the pressure. Under pressure, people talk. I shall be tuned in."

He got up, tucking three of the morning's letters into his dressing gown pocket. "Be an angel, Gorry, and sling a few shirts into a bag for me. I'm going down to South Knoll again before I leave."

"Yes?"

"Yes. I'm fussed, about that smashed car. There's something I'm missing, but don't know what. I might be wrong, but I don't think so. I want to make sure."

"You're going to be pushed for time."

He looked again at the clock.

"I know. Could you send the bag to the airport for me? I'll pick it up there."

"All right, but you're still going to be pushed, Hugo."

He disappeared and she heard the sudden fierce gush of the shower. She went into the hall and picked up the telephone, getting on to the porter.

"Jimmy, can you spare a minute to get Mr. Bishop's car round and warm the engine?"

"Big doings, miss?"

"Yes. He's going to fly out of here by centrifugal force in ten minutes and we don't want anything knocked over."

She put the receiver down and looked at it hard. This sudden trip to Monte Carlo was impulsive and in character. It didn't worry her. The woman did; the one he was going with. She'd asked him to go; he was going; simply like that. Bishop wasn't taking a week end Wendy on a sudden spree in French: there were a dozen women he'd prefer to go with, and could go with, just by asking; but Miss Gorringe couldn't quite smudge out the thought in her mind that Melody had persuaded him, when someone else couldn't have.

She knew about women, her own sex. She knew about men, how fragile they were when they wanted to be weak. But this time boy had not met girl. Bishop, who could freeze his own blood against an attack by the Amazons, had met Melody, who could turn on her sex like a flame thrower if she wanted a particular man. Last night, the woman had come here for the kill: Gorry had let her in, and Gorry knew. This morning, Hugo was in deep-freeze, a mood that excluded even herself from his isolation; he was cool, polite, particular, pointedly normal; she wasn't fooled. Bishop had a solid steel shell on him. He'd crawled into it like a hermit crab. Miss Gorringe didn't mind that. She liked it, because that was how he ought to be, with Melody in town.

But he'd booked seats on the noon plane at

three hours' notice, simply because he'd been asked.

Miss Gorringe looked at the telephone, and wondered if the steel shell were tough enough. Bishop, God knew, was a man; and men were vulnerable to one thing above all others; and just now he was right in its sights.

Sun slanted in through the roof-lights; it glinted on tools, chrome stripping, bare steel, the dark of oil. A man lay on a thin fabric mat, his legs sticking out from below the car as if his body were trapped by it and he couldn't shout. His legs were overalled. His face was staring up at the mixture of oil and mud that filmed the long, ribbed sump. A ratchet socket-spanner moved in his hand. The muscles of his hand worked cautiously against the tension of the nut; another eighth-turn could strip the thread or snap the stud, and that'd set him back a full hour to drill it out.

He finished nine, and rested his head against the mat. His neck muscles felt hot. Sweat was squeezed into the creases of his eyelids; when he closed his eyes the sweat dried in the cool air; when he opened them he saw a face framed in a triangular gap between the sump and the steering shaft. He looked sideways, rolling his head, and saw the shoes belonging to the face; they were ritzy brown suède, standing astride.

"Arthur!"

"Hello?"

"Tea up!"

"Right!"

He edged sideways, keeping his face clear of the mud-caked fender. He felt the blood ebbing away from his head as he stood up, and for a few seconds he felt dizzy. Then he kicked the switch of the inspection-lamp and looked up.

"You being seen to, sir?"

Bishop half-turned his head.

"Yes, thanks," he said, and looked back at the wreck of the Ventura alongside the other car. A week ago it had been cocked over on its side; this was the first time he had seen it upright, and it looked different. Already he had noticed a few points that had escaped him before. Abnormality in a vehicle is better revealed when it stands upright; at ninety degrees the whole machine looks abnormal.

Behind him he could hear the mechanics talking as they drank their tea. Outside the garage a car pulled up; a man went out to the pumps. The sun beat on the windows in the roof, distilling heat downwards, magnifying it and focusing it;

it was trapped in the corrugated-iron walls; the place was like an oven.

Bishop began walking round the Ventura. The blood had been cleaned away from the windshield and steering-wheel; there were fresh marks on the body where cables had chafed, hauling the two-ton load up the slope and through the trees; a ring of rope held the rear bumper clear of the ground, where a bolt had torn through the moulding. Flakes of black and white paint still clung to crevices, and a leaf, caught in the smashed remains of the headlight had shriveled and gone brown. It was the only flower on this tortured grave, and was itself dead.

The long hood was still raised above the engine, still looking like a parched, bruised mouth gaping open. Underneath it, a moth was crushed against one of the crosswise-struts. It was a smudge of dark gold. It must have hit the strut at its own speed plus the speed of the car. Its body was a little flat mess.

Bishop went on looking at the Ventura. He spent a long time on the radiator grille and the air vents for the front brakes that were let into the apron between the fenders, and he made a lot of mental photographs of the body treatment between the radiator and the front doors. There were no louvers along the sides of the hood. The edges of it came down flush with the tops of the fenders.

He looked at the moth again before he left the garage. It was a big thing originally, before the life was crushed out. It had been too big to fly through the radiator grille or the wire-mesh of the front-brake air vents. It hadn't flown in through the louvers at the side of the hood because there weren't any. It hadn't come up from underneath, because there was a flat sheet of metal surrounding the engine; it lay between the crankcase and the engine frame, and it was there to stop mud and wet and dust flying up from the road on to the engine. And moths.

Bishop looked for a long time at the moth, and knew that this was what he'd missed, before. He had talked to Melody and Sophie; he had listened to what people had said at the inquest; he had been given a very full report on David Brain by Miss Gorringe. But nothing had told him anything so surprising as did the death of this moth.

He looked at the time and found there were ten minutes left before he must make for the air-port. The works-foreman was down in the tuning shop, a long, whitewashed shed where they had a sprint-job on the lift. Bishop said to him:

"Thank you for letting me look it over again."

The man looked up, sweat on his face. It was hotter in here than in the main bay.

"You're welcome," he said.

"I didn't find anything new. All I found was one of those little puzzles that you spend all night trying to think out, and never can."

"Yes?"

Bishop nodded.

"Yes. I think it might interest you; but then you look busy."

The foreman shrugged and grinned and put down his bunch of valves and went into the main bay with Bishop. When they were standing in front of the smashed Ventura, Bishop pointed and said: "You see that moth?"

The man said: "Yes."

Bishop said: "How did it get in there?"

Straight away the man said: "Well, through the—" he bent down and looked at the grilles; then he leaned over the smashed fender and looked down at the baffle-sheet that went round the engine; then he stood back and looked at the moth.

Bishop gave him a cigarette and went out to his car. When he drove away the works-foreman was still standing in front of the Ventura; and

Bishop knew that he hadn't found the answer yet, and wasn't likely to. Because it was one of those little puzzles you spend all night trying to think out, and never can.

9th
MOVE

    ♝ RAIN HAD driven people into the bars, the terraces, casinos, and clubs. They had run from the beaches, from the tennis courts, the promenades and the gardens. Where there was no cover, the town was deserted; where there were streets, only cars moved, with the rain drumming on their roofs and spraying out from the windshield wipers. The sky was a dull steel-grey across the coast.

The rain beat down on the awning over the pavement as Bishop got out of the airport car. He helped Melody with her skirt; it was a swirl of white lace and was dedicated to summer; she gathered it round her and ran, for the rain was bouncing off the paving-stones and a small flood was rippling down to the road.

Bishop left their luggage to the porters and followed her. She swung round to face him in the hall, her teeth white in a smile.

"How nostalgic this makes me feel for Birmingham!"

"It's Manchester, where it rains."

"It is? I've never been to either."

"But you've been here."

She nodded. The smile didn't go.

"Oh, yes. With David. Twice." They wandered to the desk. "Once he was driving in the Grand Prix de Monaco—he didn't win; he smashed. The second time was when we came here to play for our lives at the tables. He did better there. We won half a million francs, enough to last us for a month." Her voice was warm, sounding softly among the marble walls, rising to the mosaic ceiling. "David was fun. He could spend money ten times faster than an exiled king, but by God he got ten times the value."

She might have been talking about someone she'd parted from, just parted from, with thanks for the memory; not that thing behind the shattered steering wheel. Bishop smiled. He said:

"This time there'll be a brake on spending, if we're together. My taxman's got a heavy frown. It's all I can do to lift it."

She stood close to him.

"I don't want to spend money, Hugo. I just want to be away from the world, here with you."

He moved to the desk.

"Away from the world, in Monte?"

"From the other world. This one's isolated. It's out of the past, a gay old ghost with an overdraft tucked underneath its arm. We shan't see anyone shoot themselves at the tables: no one can afford a gun."

He thought, while he was signing the book, that already she had changed. They hadn't come far: a few hours in a plane; but she had lost ninety per cent of her tension. Was that because she was out of the "other world," or out of reach of Struve? He couldn't decide.

She signed in after him. From London she had booked a double room, and he had canceled it, booking two singles. She had taken it well, and he knew why. What power she believed she had with him lay in herself, not in the mere proximity of walls.

"I'm going up to rest, Hugo."

"All right. See you at dinner?"

"No, before. Six, in the terrace bar." She swung her head once before she left him, looking back. "Unless you get bored."

"If I do, I shan't disturb you. It wouldn't be fair."

She said nothing, but walked away. Bishop

saw that half the men in here were not attending to their wives, their mistresses, their newspapers, their porters. When Melody walked, people watched. He waited, just as they did, until she reached the lift; then he rested one arm on the reception desk again, and idly turned the pages of the book.

He had to go back three months before he found the name. *Mr. and Mrs. D. A. Brain. Suite II. British.*

She had suggested this hotel, saying she knew it and that it was good. He had known why, and the book had confirmed it. They were still moving in the wake of the dead; and he was satisfied. He was here to find out about Brain; and here they were near him again.

At six the terrace bar was filling up. People were coming in for cocktails before late dinner. Bishop had taken a sun-chair in the corner five minutes ago.

With a Cinzano on the round wicker table he looked down over the balustrade of the terrace. Below was a purple mist of bougainvillea, drifting across white walls; the canvas of yachts dappled the harbor waters, blossoming like oleanders in the blue; for the rain had stopped, hours ago, and Monte Carlo was a cliché in color again, a hackneyed phrase, a rain-washed copy of a million picture postcards that said: this is Paradise—you should be here—wonderful food—must catch the post now. . . .

The Englishman thought: once this place was beautiful, with the buildings couched in the hill's foot and the bay like a blue lawn, smooth under the sun. Yet except for a few of the new hotels with their sparse-looking American architecture the place was the same as when it had been beautiful. Now it was too familiar. The picture postcards had made scenes like this one tawdry without touching them or altering one petal of these flowers; the postcards and the travelogues in Technicolor, the brochures and the tourism-pictures, the airline folders and the outpoured mediocrity of a hundred unoriginal commercial artists had taken Monte Carlo off the map and put it on glossy paper, and it was two-dimensional and flat.

By seven o'clock the terrace was almost deserted again. Bishop had not moved. He sat watching a little Greek who sat on a stool brooding over his glass and something in his soul. Waiters were in idle groups behind the bar and along the balustrade. A thin, grey-faced man from a travel agency was going down the steps to look for more people who might—unlike the

Englishman in the corner—be persuaded to go on to Italy or Spain. A pedigree poodle, a king's or perhaps a croupier's, was sniffing about among the tables to pick up its master's trail.

Melody had not come by ten past seven. Bishop left, and had dinner alone. Later he wandered down to the Casino, as others were doing. Like the little ivory balls that went spinning into the wheels, people gravitated to the salons and settled there to live their night by numbers, win or lose.

The place was less than half-full when he took his ticket and went in. Melody, if she were here, would not be playing craps or baccara or trente-et-quarante; he made for the Salons Privés, where the gambling had an added quality that was subtle and scarcely realized: the visual hypnosis of the wheel. It spun, and while it spun you could watch nothing else. Almost more important than the fate of the ball and your stake, that silent thing must spin. You were a kid, happy go lucky until it stopped.

At this hour the people were intent on their play. They were the regulars, the inveterates; they were not playing for show; they were playing for money. Later the other kinds would come: the duchesses and the dilettanti, the touts and the gigolos, the people who would stake

their next week's living on the big man at
the end of the table who liked them young,
or the brown-skinned woman half-way along
who hired and fired her ex-college chauffeurs
twice a month but wasn't mean to them. These
were the people who would come to watch the
play, to select a sucker or an audience, to place
their bets much less on chance than on their
chances. This was the other side of the picture
postcard; it anything, it was more honest.

Bishop played for an hour and lost a few francs
more than he won, then gave up his seat to a pale
American girl. She thanked him with a smile
that was forced out of her, and when she put
down her chips he wondered if they had cost
her everything she had, or more than that. Her
tension was palpable in the jerk of her hands
and the febrile flick of her eyes.

He wandered out to a bar and sat down by the
wall, facing the doors. He had already seen Melody, but she hadn't looked up. She was at a table
with a big, bland-faced man. Daily massages had
smoothed out most of the character in his face
but nothing could alter the eyes. They were a
quiet hermit's eyes; they looked out from deep
inside a shell; if people watched him for too long
he looked down, and the smooth, hooded lids cut
him off from the contact and he was alone again.

She said to him: "You look well, Geoffrey. But then you always did."

"You look ravishing. But then you always will."

They were drinking Americanos. He added with a mouth-smile: "But you've changed, a little. Not in your looks."

"How then?"

"You're even less in love with life than when I saw you last."

"You mean I hate it even more."

He shrugged.

"It's nothing to do with me," he said.

"You haven't changed at all, Geoffrey. Nothing is ever to do with you, is it? What's it feel like, to be marooned on that island of yours after all these years?"

"Not marooned. Safely ensconced. I'm a recluse, not an exile." He studied his square, manicured nails for a moment. "It feels very good. Sometimes—but rarely—I feel I'm missing something. That's all."

"Life?"

"No. Living. But these days—" he shrugged again, looking round the room.

"Geoffrey," she said, "you're running to fat. Did you know?"

"Running to type. My father was the same. He played squash, tennis, golf, for thirty years. In his spare time he rode, swam, climbed mountains, and shot game. He was fifteen stone when he died—of a fatty heart."

She smiled whitely.

"That won't ever happen to you, darling. You're like the lion in the Wizard of Oz—but don't let it bother you. Hearts are expensive, and no longer trumps."

"You've had a bad time. Unlike you, Melody."

"You're wrong. I've had a good time. Nobody's broken my heart, because I haven't got one either." She splayed her fingers and wedged the glass stem between them. "I fell in love with someone, a little while ago. And he's mine for life."

She didn't glance up when he spoke. He sounded surprised.

"I'm glad for you."

"And astonished."

"A little, yes. I never thought I'd hear you talk about 'falling in love.' "

"I don't talk about it. I simply mentioned it as a background fill-in. And don't ask why it seems to have made me hate life more than ever. It hasn't. I just do. Since I saw you last I've had six more months of living—the thing you sometimes miss." She looked up. "Don't fret your soul about it. You can still call it as good as a mile."

"Poor Melody . . . I wonder how much you'd give to be on my island that you so despise. . . . "

"Nothing. Not with you there."

A muscle in his face moved; he looked down; the smile did not go: it was a habit of his mouth.

She had lost interest in him. She was watching the people coming in, going out. Bishop said:

"Hello."

She glanced up.

"Hello, Hugo." He was looking politely at the bland, sunburned man. She said: "Geoffrey de Whett—Hugo Bishop, two friends of mine."

De Whett got up, looking at Bishop from the depths of his shell. He said: "Will will you join us?"

Bishop looked at Melody. "Please," she said, without much feeling. They sat down and de Whett signaled a waiter. When the drinks were ordered he said: "Have you been playing?"

Melody was watching the doors. Bishop was watching a man drinking absinthe at the bar. They both turned their heads to de Whett. He was looking at Bishop.

"Yes," said Bishop, "but not seriously."

De Whett smiled. "*Sur deux douzaines?*"

"Well, not quite. *Carré.*"

"Have you seen the Duke of Velaña?"

"With the two little bodyguard chaps?"

De Whett nodded. "Yes. He's been in there an hour, playing *en plein*. When I left there he was doubling in thousands. If you like we'll go back in ten minutes, to see him win."

"You've fixed the wheel?" said Melody. She was touching Bishop's hand on the table. De Whett was watching it.

"No. Nobody has to. Velaña always wins, and it always interests me to watch a couple of castles and a possible Derby winner changing hands on the spin of a marble."

"How does he always win?" said Melody.

De Whett looked away from her hand. He said: "By doubling. If you go on doubling, you must always win. Last week he had to double seventeen times before his number came up. His original stake was a thousand francs—the price of a meager lunch. His return was a hundred and thirty million."

Bishop said: "What happens if he has to double as far as twenty?"

"He has to stake a thousand million francs."

"That would be interesting to see," said Melody. De Whett nodded.

"Yes, it is." He smiled sadly. "I don't know how much the management pays him for always winning—they say it's enough to rent him a villa in the town. That's cheap, because he's magnificent publicity, and others follow his numbers also *en plein*." He shrugged. "These days, very few will touch it, without that kind of encouragement."

Bishop inclined his head.

"A nice story," he said, "however obviously untrue."

De Whett shrugged again. "Some people believe it, and to me it's worth a drink. On principle, I never lie for nothing; and like the Duke of Velaña, I must live."

He excused himself after ten minutes and Melody said:

"Poor Geoffrey. He never quite comes off."

"What's he afraid of?"

"Being winkled out of his shell. In a way, he's David's opposite. The two of them used to meet here sometimes, and it was interesting to watch."

Bishop said gently, "But then it was always interesting to watch David . . . anywhere. Wasn't it?"

Her eyes went cold.

"Yes, it was. Anywhere at all."

"But more especially when he was talking to his opposite, naturally."

She didn't look away. "You're talking on the surface. What about?"

"De Whett. He makes me curious. Unless it's

too personal—what made you marry him?"

The dark pupils expanded momentarily in the pale cold blue; that was all.

"Have you seen Geoffrey before?" she asked. Her hands were perfectly still on the table.

"No."

"Who told you I was his wife?"

"I forget."

"That's inconvenient, Hugo, because I'd like to know."

"Let me help you. There can't be many people who could tell me, can there?"

"Why not?"

"Wasn't it one of those rather romantic escapades with a fast car through the mountains and a simple priest?"

She said nothing. Her head was poised beautifully and her eyes were steady. He had seen a cheetah gaze at him like this from behind bars, and with as little affection. He waited for her to say something, but in a moment she merely looked away, and finished the drink in her glass.

He said: "You can't hope to bring me to a place where you've been so many times before and not expect me to run into friends of yours."

"You've been making inquiries about me here?"

"Well, no. Information wasn't solicited."

She said: "If you've run into friends of mine here, it didn't take you long."

"You've so many friends."

"Fewer now, I think."

He lit a cigarette for her. "If you remember, Melody, we came here on certain terms. On the crest of a wave, I think you said. Underneath, it's deep."

She looked at him through the smoke of her cigarette.

"You said I was dangerous," she said. "It's taken me a long time to find it's mutual. In a way, it excites me."

He nodded.

"Danger would do that to you, Melody. Danger in whatever form: the mere spectacle—boxing, motor-racing, bullfighting—or the recent presence of it: such as the still-warm wreck of a smash—or the threat of it to yourself. Emotionally, you've got to have danger; otherwise you'd blow your top."

"Succinct summing-up of Case Number 345. See Chapter on How to Split the Id."

Bishop didn't smile. He asked:

"But you know how right or how wrong I am. You know yourself. And you're beginning to know me."

"I think I am, yes. I'm losing some illusions—less about you than about myself. I kept you waiting an hour in the terrace bar this evening; you knew my room number; I'd told you to come up if you got bored. And you never came."

He said, "But I wasn't bored."

She leaned forward, resting her left arm along the table. Her right hand was bunched on the table between her glass and his hand. Suddenly she flicked her finger, stinging him. She was smiling. She said softly:

"I'd love to hurt you, Hugo."

"Out of what?"

"The hell of it."

Their eyes were lightly on each other's and they were both smiling a little. He murmured: "Don't look now, but your fetish is showing."

"No, it's not my fetish. Not many women are sadists."

"But they bite."

Softly and quickly she said: "I wish to God that in your long, thin, pale-faced, priggish sort of way you weren't so infuriatingly attractive. How do you do it?"

"By not accepting deep-purple invitations."

Between her white small teeth she said: "Why didn't you come up to my room?"

"Lifts frighten me."

"Afraid of falling?"

"No. Of hitting the ground."

"Have you ever fallen? Ever? For anyone?"

"Well," he said, and as he spoke his smile slowly went, "there was a girl I met, a few years ago. Her name was Polly and she let me hold her hand in the dark—we were waiting to pinch a sack of coke from a siding in Bootle Station—and she—"

"I was there an hour," she said with a sudden fierce rawness in her voice. "When you didn't come, I didn't believe it."

"Dear heart," said Bishop patiently, "we've talked about this before. I thought we had it all worked out. I still don't know your real reason for asking me to come here with you; but I told you mine. I want to know what killed David Brain. Until I've found out, I'm not interested in anything else."

After a long time she said in a cold, flat tone:

"It was a fractured skull."

He looked at her steadily. He said:

"Let's not be childish about this. It wasn't the fracture that killed him. It wasn't the speed he was doing or the slide his car went into. It wasn't the drink in him. It was an impulse in someone's mind that smashed the life out of his body. He was killed with intent. I want to know whose."

She watched him, calm and still. Her hand was just touching his. It was cold, as cold as it had been when he had helped her up the dark earth slope between the moonlit trees.

"I want to know who murdered him," he said.

Her eyes didn't change. Bishop looked up. De Whett stood with his hands in his pockets and the mouth-smile on his face.

He said: "Velaña's won. You should have seen it. He took twelve million francs."

10th
MOVE

BISHOP HAD breakfast on the balcony the next morning. Miss Gorringe's air-mail letter was on the table in front of him. From the brief economical sentences he drew two clearer pictures: one of Everett Struve, the other of Melody Carr.

Melody had been born in two rooms over a seamen's loan office in Rio de Janiero twenty-eight years ago. Her mother kept a café. Her mother's husband, a mercantile captain, had gone down with his ship off Chile two years before Melody was born. Her father was unknown. Melody Carr—then Martha Retzel—went on the stage in her teens and left Rio for England when she was twenty. No trace now of her mother. Melody crossed with a fifth-rate dancing show and was kicked out after a month in London because of an affair involving two men in the company, both married. No further trace until five years ago when she appeared as a cabaret singer at the Black Orchid. In an incident between the manager and her agent there was a violent fight; the manager was killed; a charge of manslaughter was brought and proved against the agent, who served three years in prison. Just before he was released, Melody went to Italy. No trace for eighteen months or so. Last year she was in Paris, living with a man named de Whett. She came back to London before the winter, and trace of de Whett was lost.

Everett Struve: very little further information available. American-born, he did not serve in War II, but was mixed up in an F.B.I. inquiry concerning sale of chemicals to an Italian combine in 1944. Nothing was proved. He was injured in a car accident just after the war and was two or three months in hospital. He was in England, representing a chemical firm, six months ago, and stayed nearly three before returning to the U.S.

Bishop memorized the essentials and as soon as he had finished breakfast sent a cable to Miss Gorringe:

Please check Struve's arrival date in England, said to be four days ago. Check details of his car accident: was he driving? Check whereabouts of ex-convict agent. Don't let Her Highness run out of mice.

He left the cable office and found a branch of General-Auto Distributors in Boulevard Saint-Denis. They showed him a Ventura. He told the man: "I've just been looking over one of these in England. I like the extra thought spent on detail."

The hood was raised. The man was pleased to show off these "high luxury points." (He quoted from the brochure.)

"One thing that interested me," Bishop said, "was the way the engine's sealed off from below. Don't you have trouble getting the hot air and fumes away?"

"That's taken care of." The man pointed. "Those two wide slots behind the block are specially-designed fume-escape ducts, and the driving compartment's lined on this side with baffling material. Steel-spun fabric with a sandwich of asbestos. It stops fumes, heat and road dust."

"I see. That's what impresses me—the attention to detail. I wondered if the model I saw over there had been specially fitted-up with these refinements."

"People ask that, but it isn't so. This car's four years old, like the one you saw, and it's in production trim. We're proud of it."

"You should be."

"I'd like to give you a run in her, if you've the time."

Bishop hadn't the time. He took away a brochure and studied it in his hotel. It didn't show him anything more than he had seen, but he had seen enough. His one-man inquest on the death of the moth was closed, but the small, smashed body was a vital witness, as late as this, to the death of the man whose Ventura had sent him off Knoll Hill to his grave.

Bishop went down to the terrace. Coming into the hotel ten minutes ago he had seen Melody there. She was still there now. She was in a sunchair and she looked more like a colored picture of temptation incarnate than a colored picture of temptation incarnate would look.

"Hugo, this is Dominic."

Dominic stood up. He was a tall, brownskinned man with good shoulders and gentle hands. His eyes were pale, like something semiopaque with the sun shining from behind. Two white grapes, but thinking. They were thinking eyes. Bishop thought women must go mad when they saw someone like this.

"How do you do?" His accent was not any one country's, any more than his face. He was a European; that was all one could say.

Bishop said hello and sat down. It was getting a habit to find Melody sitting at a table with a man, and to join them. He wondered if she were doing it deliberately, out of pique, but changed his mind. As a plant needed sunlight, this woman needed men. Just to be near. It was obvious but odd, because if Bishop had found out one certain thing about Martha Retzel, it was that she hated men. From their guts to their graves.

"Dominic is a diver," she said.

Bishop said: "Yes?"

Dominic nodded politely. "Yes."

Bishop wanted to ask the obvious question: "What do you dive for?"—but an odd quirk in him half-expected the man to say "For cover," and burst out laughing. It was such a weird thing to say, simply: "Dominic is a diver."

Bishop said: "Pearls, or just fun?"

As if he had forgotten the subject, the man swung his leonine head.

"Anything," he said.

Melody nodded. "I'm going to watch him today. In the harbor. He's going to dive for me."

Bishop said: "Really?"

Suddenly Dominic smiled. "I don't know why

I have been asked to do it. What is there to see?
There is nothing to bring up from the harbor but
rusty fishing tackle."

Bishop knew what Melody would see.
Strength, grace, endurance, rhythm—a glimpse
of the son of Poseidon in his own element.

"Have you been diving all your life?" said Bishop.

"Yes, all my life. Under the water, I am happy."
He smiled again. "I am a mistake. I should have
been born as a fish."

Bishop liked the man. He could now place the
odd pale quality of his eyes: they were deep
green water with the sun somewhere above.
They had taken on the quality of his favorite
element.

Melody was looking at Bishop. Almost as if
Dominic were not there she said: "He's been telling me. He dives for anything—sponge, pearls,
riches in wrecks, unusual specimens of marine
life that he catches for naturalists, anything. He
runs terrific risks."

Dominic looked a little embarrassed. He said
with his quick, clean grin: "Yes, there are almost
as many risks as there are when we cross the
street in Paris."

Bishop smiled. "Then your number's practically up."

"My number?"

Melody said: "He means that's pretty dangerous."

Even in the way she said the word "dangerous" there was the hint of her pleasure.

Dominic shook his head. "It is really very safe. Sometimes if you are in the Pacific there is seaweed floating, and it is difficult to cut through with your knife—the stems are often as thick as your own arm. And there are sharks, of course, but if you shout at them they usually go away."

Melody said: "Shout?"

"Yes. The noise frightens them. But you lose much of your breath, shouting, and must go up quickly then." He shrugged. "You have to dodge them, like taxis—and it is no good shouting at taxis. I prefer the sharks, all except the Gray Nurses." He talked slowly, reminiscently. Bishop judged that he always talked like this about the underwater. He was down there most of the time; even now.

"What are they?"

Melody was fascinated. Bishop thought: this time she's landed a big one, a big beautiful one in dangerous waters.

"The Gray Nurses you find off New Zealand. Their skin is the silver-grey of the nurses' uniforms there. Unlike the human ones, these have no mercy. There is a foolish legend: they always get their man. You can shout at them, but they do not scare, and when you have lost your breath and rise quickly to the surface they follow you. Their speed is very great and the shadow of your boat—even if it is a large one—does not frighten them. They follow you always and there is a silver flush in the water as they turn over for the kill."

Melody's voice grated; it came from a dry throat.

"You've met one?"

"Yes. It was off one of the islands. We were only in a few fathoms and the water was clear. The Gray Nurse was there to find bell fish. It saw me and followed me up. The other man was beside me. All we could do was to rip at the water with our Knives and try to swim to the boat at the same time. From the boat the Maoris were yelling and throwing fish spears and lead weights and everything they could find, to frighten away the shark. But a Gray Nurse is like a fighting bull: it fears nothing. I reached the boat safely and they pulled me on board. Behind me the water was foaming red and white. The red was blood. The other man was my brother; it was my brother's blood."

Melody could not look away from the strong,

dark face. Bishop watched her reflection in his glass. Dominic was looking down over the mist of bougainvillea to the small, blue harbor. His pupils were points.

"There is no time to think of one's brother when death is laughing in one's face. They killed the fish, too. A spear went through her eye. Later we saw her mate, a big male." His head moved; he looked slowly from the harbor to the horizon. "The lonely mate will search the oceans until he dies of old age. They cannot recognize death."

Bishop felt Melody shiver. Dominic looked at them and suddenly smiled.

"But there are no Gray Nurses in these waters. I will dive in the harbor and fetch you some rusty tackle, or a cheap glass ring—tossed there by an outraged lover when she learned the price."

"This morning?" Her voice was rough.

"If you wish."

She swung her head to Bishop. "Come and watch too."

"All right, I'd like to."

In the afternoon Bishop partnered de Whett in a game of tennis at the Club d'Eté. They played for an hour and then sat with iced Colas on the

veranda. De Whett was worried about his waist-
line.

"Melody says I'm running to fat. Do you think
so, Bishop?"

"What d'you want me to tell you?"

"Tell me no."

"No, I wouldn't say you were."

De Whett grimaced and for a little while
watched the courts. At last he said: "Where is
she now?"

"Who?"

The bland face was turned.

"Melody. Didn't you come here together?"

"Yes. I don't know where she is. With Dominic,
I'd hazard."

"Dominic Feurte?"

"Is that his name? The diver."

"The same. A good man. I don't know what he's
doing in this diamond-littered dust bowl. He's a
nature boy."

"Possibly he's here for the same reason as you."

De Whett smiled with his mouth. He asked:
"Which is?"

Bishop shrugged. "How can I say? But it might
be his reason too."

"I'm here," de Whett said slowly, "to watch people. I like doing it. I've a friend-proof plate glass
wigwam that I pull down over my ears and watch

people through. Nothing personal—I'm enjoying your company. But the scene is interesting in a chilling kind of way. You know how you watch a raised patch of sand that gets smaller as the tide comes in? It's like that. This world here was never very big. Now it's begun to shrink."

Bishop half-closed his eyes, watching the rhythm of brown limbs, the flutter of white linen, the stinging sweep of the rackets, the flight of the balls.

"You mean the money's running out?" he said.

"More than the money. The fun. People used to come to places like this for fun. That was good, and they got it. They paid, but fun is worth paying for. Now they come here for asylum, for escape. They come running. The taxman's after their money; the government's after their liberty; the hydrogen bomb's after their lives. They try to forget it, while they're here, but they can't. Diamonds are getting smaller. Pearl-chokers are shrinking until the countesses gasp for air. The news gets worse—the news from everywhere except here; and this place isn't news anymore. It's a playground that's turning into a graveyard. Or worse—a museum. Better dead than just gone." He picked up his glass and drank.

"People look happy enough," Bishop said. "What about those down there?"

"Oh, *tennis*. One-half per cent of them play tennis—or swim, or surf ride. Good, clean fun. The rest of them drift from one bar to the next, from roulette to baccara, from bromide to bismuth. Like I do—before you wish you could say it. Why not? It's faith-healing under self-hypnosis. As a phase of society, interesting to watch."

"I should envy your detachment."

"But you don't. You're not one of these people anyway. You're here to do something. Melody was telling me. She never said what."

Bishop said: "I'm here to hold an inquest."

For an instant the man's smile touched his eyes.

"So our reasons are the same."

"Not quite. This is on one man, not a social world."

"Is that so? What man?"

"David Brain."

In the background a slim girl served a fault and her arm swung up again. In the foreground, de Whett's face lost none of its bland immobility.

"Brain," he said. "I heard about him. But the inquest is over, surely?"

"The official one. This is private."

De Whett looked at him obliquely.

"And personal?"

"Only in that I was concerned in the smash."

"You were the motorist, that's right. Melody told me."

"She talked about the smash?"

"A little. I'd met Brain, so I was interested." He put his hands together, pressing the palms and turning them slowly as if he were rubbing tobacco. "You weren't satisfied with the verdict of accidental death?"

"At the time, perhaps. Not since."

For minutes de Whett didn't speak. He appeared to be watching the courts. A waiter took away their glasses. The *thwock* of the balls echoed against the wall of the veranda, hollow and staccato.

"Have you reached a new verdict, of your own?"

"Not quite."

"But nearly?"

"Perhaps."

De Whett looked at him directly and asked: "And what does it look like it's going to be? Same as the coroner's?"

"No. Murder."

"Is that so? Against whom?"

"Persons unknown."

"Persons . . . plural!"

"Yes."

"This is interesting. And are you going to find out their names if you can—these persons unknown?"

"I expect so."

"You take a lot on yourself," de Whett said gently.

"I like it." Bishop tilted his head back and started filling his meerschaum, not looking at de Whett. "In a way, you and I are both interested in the same thing. People. You've got a floodlight— you see the crowd. I use a spotlight—I see the individual in clear focus." He zipped the tobacco pouch and put it away. "I expect that's why you say you're interested in my little inquest. Not for any personal reason."

He struck a match and watched de Whett's profile as it was half-turned. There was the shine of sweat on his smooth face. The sun beat down, beat up from the veranda floor. On the nearest court a man threw down his racket and lay flat on his back, exhausted. After what seemed minutes Bishop heard de Whett's voice coming ruminatively:

"Brain was a better subject for your kind of study than mine, Bishop. He was an individual. You could focus on a man like him. I didn't know him well, but I met him three or four times when he came here with Melody. I liked him. He was man-sized. Other people liked him too. He was very popular."

Bishop said slowly: "Yes. People have told me that. Everyone seemed to like him a great deal. Except two of them."

The bland head swiveled.

"The persons unknown?"

"Yes. And even when I find them, I think they'll be among the people who've told me how much they liked David Brain. For a popular type, he had a lot of pressure put on him."

De Whett shrugged. He said:

"No man's loved by all the world." He squinted idly at the smoke that was drifting in the sunshine from the bowl of the meerschaum. "You know Melody very well?"

"Hardly at all."

"She's like him, in a lot of ways. Like Brain. A hell of an individual. I suppose that's why they got on so well."

"Individualists usually don't. Their personalities are too strong and too set."

"That's right, I suppose, but this could have been an exception. They made a nice pair of people. You know sometimes you meet two people who are together, and you have to stop and look at them because you know you've seen something rare. A kind of living harmony. You can see it in the way they look at each other, hear it when they talk—I don't mean the cow-eyed, dream-heavy, sugar-coated, newly wed type of premature dotage you see in honeymoon hotels. I mean harmony, the real thing. The deep chord." He looked at Bishop with a sudden quirk. "For me, that sounds out of character."

"Yes?"

"You'd think so, if you knew me. I've never kidded myself there's much harmony in the world. Not deep. There's plenty of it on show, and you can hear it wherever you go. All smiles and sentiment and warmth of humanity. But it's light music, played on strings." The quirk of amusement faded from his face. "And strings have tension. They snap."

Bishop said: "Do you believe in anything at all?"

"Yes. I believe in people. Real people: human, weak, struggling, suffering people who do their best to wring the neck out of life before it wrings theirs. I'd rather believe in them than in any rose-colored peep show that you can see whenever you want to, for a penny a time. Melody's like that, too. So—I think—was Brain."

Suddenly Bishop decided to say: "Did you ever meet him in England?"

De Whett said: "No. I haven't been to England

156

for a long time. Not since Melody was there. And that was my reason. She's the most wonderful girl in the world, but if you want to go to hell, she knows the way."

"So did Brain."

Gently: "Yes. I wonder they didn't go together."

"They weren't far apart. They were on the same road."

"You think she killed him?" asked de Whett.

Bishop smiled. He said evenly: "There are a lot of ways of killing someone. Most of them are subtle. She's not a very subtle person. If she'd wanted to kill the only man she loved, I'd say she would have just shot him down."

De Whett didn't say anything. Bishop asked:

"Wouldn't you think so?"

"Yes." His voice had suddenly gone flat. He watched the courts as if the play interested him. Bishop said:

"She's throwing an intimate party tonight. I believe you're coming."

"Yes." The bland face didn't turn.

Bishop got up slowly, dropping a scatter of ash on to his chair.

"I'll see you again, then, tonight."

De Whett glanced up. His eyes were screwed to slits against the sun. It broke the smoothness of his face and he looked less of a mask.

"Bishop, I don't know much about anything that goes on in people. I don't let myself. There's too much pushing down of privacy. One half of the world doesn't know how to let the other half live. But I'd say this: Monte Carlo's an odd place to come to, to meddle with murder."

Bishop shrugged. He said: "Murder's where you find it. And sometimes it's a long way from home. See you tonight."

De Whett watched him walk away; and when the tall, slight figure had gone from the veranda, he turned his head and looked again at the tennis players. There was no expression on the smooth, tanned face, and nothing in the eyes except the reflection of the tiny images in white that hit the balls back and forth, back and forth across the nets.

11^{*th*}

MOVE

♟ THE AIR was close. Windows were open, but they just let warm air in. The air moved only when people moved. It was tangible; it brushed the face; it was like the music that Melody had put on the record player: sweet, and a little stifling. But people did not mind; they were talking, listening. Mostly talking.

Dominic Feurte stood with his legs slightly astride, leonine head held forward as he listened to a girl in gold shoes and white shoulders. He looked out of place here among the women and flowers and music, like a hunter trapped by doves. He was smiling at the girl. She talked very fast and was looking at someone with little jerks of her head. She looked quite in place here. She looked as if she were assessing the company for Dominic's benefit, stripping the women to show their age, the men to show their income. To any who knew the man, Dominic was clearly thinking about deep-sea sponge.

Melody was watching him. She had on a white sheath and sandals. She stood a few yards from Dominic, who glanced at her now and then with his luminous eyes. Neither smiled to the other. At this moment—barely an hour after the party had begun—nobody happened to be standing between them. To anyone who knew of them, it was clear that whoever happened to move between them would be burned by the current.

De Whett was drinking hard, perched on a window sill and talking to someone outside on the moonlit veranda. De Whett was not getting drunk. He could sit there for hours like that, a new glass always in his hand, without getting drunk. He would simply become, very gradually, made of wood. He would see you, answer you, get a drink, laugh at your story, promise to ring you tomorrow, respect every requirement of a fellow guest. A lifeless automaton carved out of smooth brown wood. Tomorrow, he would be the only guest you couldn't call to mind.

Bishop was by the phonograph. He said he would keep the music going when the automatic change got rid of its sequence of ten records. When the music stopped, no one would notice. When he started it again, no one would notice. But that was why he was near the phonograph. He held a Pimms, and a man who sold oil pipe lines was talking to him about oil pipe lines and how hard it was to scrape a living out of selling them. His Hispano-Suiza was parked outside and his wife was at his elbow. The girl talking to Feurte had assessed the woman's ring at five figures, sterling.

In the French doors was the Duke of Velaña. He was a small, dark, cheerful man with an eagle nose and bright eyes. He had been laughing a good deal, was absolutely sober, and had been looking across at his hostess for some time now. He had asked her to stay at one of his smaller castles when she had a few days to spare; she had refused; he would ask her again tonight. It had not been difficult for Melody to persuade him to come to her party; she had invited him herself, and not by card.

There were a dozen other people, some in the room, some on the tiny veranda. From here the terraces ran down to a hill road that led to the town. The town was a jewel box spilled at the edge of the dark velvet sea; only if one could forget the picture postcards was it possible to stand here on the veranda and see it simply as a rather charming little town, with lamplit streets and a few ships riding in the bay.

The moonlight was faintly blue, tinged by some unknown medium, perhaps the clarity of air alone. Few women were on the veranda; the pinkish glow of the room lights was kinder to their skin; they were the sort of women who knew it, and watched such a point with care. Also they watched their hostess, and their hostess, and their men.

When Everett Struve arrived the only one who noticed him was Bishop; for Bishop had been waiting. He had seen Struve twice this evening, once at the cable office and once at the Casino. It had seemed a matter of time before he found this hotel, and Melody's name in the book.

He came in alone, in a dinner jacket. Before the door was closed he had seen Melody, but didn't go straight over to her. Bishop thought it might be that Struve was not sure whose party it was. He just stayed by the door, looking round the room quietly. When he saw Bishop he stopped moving his head. Bishop eased himself between the people and reached the door and said:

"Hello, Struve."

Struve looked at him dead-faced for a moment

and then said: "Melody introduced us, but I forget your name."

Bishop smiled.

"That's all right," he said. Struve knew his name very well. Unless Melody had told anyone else where she was going yesterday morning, Miss Gorringe was the only person who could have passed on the information to Struve. To get that information, he would have had to telephone the name of Bishop.

"You're a fraction late for the party," Bishop said nicely. "What delayed you?"

The American's eyes went stony.

"I wasn't delayed. I wasn't invited. I'm crashing. Whose party is it—hers?"

Bishop looked at a slight loss, his eyes moving over the people. "There are so many women here. Which particular 'her' do you mean?"

"Don't bother."

"All right. I'm sort of co-host. What will you drink?"

"I'd like Scotch."

"Good. Come over here and we'll tell you who the others are." They squeezed between people and the wall. Bishop glanced up from the decanter as Melody caught sight of Struve. He stood quietly and went a bit pale. Bishop thought it was anger. She blinked her eyes and then smiled very brilliantly; it was a nice double-take.

"Darling Everett!"

"Hello," he said. "I'd like to talk to you."

Bishop poured three fingers and handed the glass to Struve. Melody said: "I'd like to talk to you too, darling. What are you doing in Monte— I didn't know you were coming over?"

"I came to see you."

"How lovely. If I'd known you were going to be so sweet I would have invited you up here. As it is, you're very welcome."

Bishop was smiling across at de Whett. De Whett was watching him, and miming gently with his hands as if he were studying something under a microscope.

"Thank you," Struve said. "I'd like to talk to you alone somewhere." His voice was a monotone.

She said: "I'll think about it, tomorrow. Have you met everybody? You know Hugo—"

"I'm not interested in everybody. I'd like to talk to you. Now." He didn't touch his drink. The music swung out with a lush rhythm from the phonograph. Voices had become high, brittle, disjointed. Velaña was moving slowly from the French windows towards Melody, Struve and Bishop. Dominic Feurte was looking all the time at Melody. She said with a meekness that surprised Bishop:

"Please don't be so demanding, Everett. I can't talk to you now—"

"You can come back."

She glanced at Bishop with a sudden appeal, then looked down at her glass. "Not now, Everett. Not tonight."

Struve said: "Now. But preferably of your own free will."

Feurte was standing beside her. Velaña was half-way through the crowd, laughing to someone as he passed them. Bishop said quietly to Struve:

"I'll take you round now, Struve, to meet the others."

Struve didn't look away from Melody as he spoke.

"Would you mind just going away, Bishop?"

Melody glanced up at the immense Feurte and smiled, nervous-eyed. She said, "Everett, this is Dominic Feurte. Dominic—Everett Struve."

The two men looked at each other. Struve nodded. Feurte smiled. Bishop touched Struve's arm gently and murmured:

"Bring your drink along with you."

Melody said softly, "Thank you, Hugo."

Bishop couldn't for the moment think why she was acting so completely out of character, because the moment was becoming tricky. If he had to get Struve out of the room by force, the American would make a good fight of it. He was nearly as big as Feurte and had an adamant jaw. In this little room it wasn't possible for two men to start scrapping without killing half the people off as a side issue. Bishop thought of asking Feurte to help things along by hog-tying Struve between them very quickly and hustling him through the crowd before anything was noticed. Most of the people had second vision coming on, and only a few of them would pay any attention. On the other hand, that wouldn't be fair to Struve, with the odds doubled.

He kept on looking at Melody. Bishop said:

"Come along and meet people, Struve." He smiled nicely. "I insist."

Struve turned his head. He said with a voice that dropped the words out like stones, "People don't insist, with me. I'd like you to go away now."

Melody said something softly to Dominic, but Struve was concentrating on Bishop now. Bishop gripped his arm in a way that looked friendly to anyone who was watching. De Whett was watching; there might be others.

"I'm afraid I can't go away. If you don't want to meet the others, you're not really enjoying the party, so I'll take you outside. Otherwise you might stop others enjoying it too."

The man's face went pale again, and this time Bishop knew it was anger.

"I don't want to spoil anyone's fun, Bishop. I'm here to see Melody."

"All right. Let's just go outside for a minute to get the air. Then if you feel like coming back, you can see her."

It had been said lightly and in a tone that was almost friendly, but the issue was quite clear. Bishop was still gripping Struve's arm, and felt the other hand move with a jerk that shivered his whole body. Struve couldn't have hoped to swing a blow with any real aim in this throng, and for a moment Bishop couldn't see what was going on, until he glanced at Dominic Feurte. Feurte was looking hard at the American. Struve had brought his free arm back to swing it and Feurte had stopped him. They were both holding him now.

Melody murmured: "Dominic—" and broke off as Struve wrenched his arms free. His glass hit the floor. Bishop put his own down quickly and braced himself but Feurte was chopping the edge of his hand down as Struve's arm came up.

The moment for hustling him quietly out was past, and Bishop thought it was a pity, because

although people were gently ginned up they
were all behaving very well.

Feurte put a loose hook across Struve's jaw
line, the best he could manage in the confined
space, but it only grazed the skin and tilted the
head a few inches. A woman gave a little polite
scream and the talk broke down. In the three-
second silence of surprise there came a snapping
noise as knuckles glanced off bone, and then the
buzz of alarm came and people began crowding
back. Two or three had their drinks knocked out
of their hands.

Bishop felt there was still a little time to get
Struve out and go on with the party. If he were
allowed to go really wild the whole evening
would break up and a lot of people would be
hurt. So Bishop managed to cut a strong hand-
blow against the inside of Struve's arm, edge-on
and just below the shoulder. He touched exactly
the right spot, and Struve's arm dropped out of
action, paralyzed. Bishop heard his breath grunt
as Feurte snapped his other arm back and tucked
it at right angles behind him.

The people kept back against the walls. Considering how crowded the room had looked before Struve had come, there was a lot of clear
space in the middle now. Struve was saying
something, but Feurte put some pressure on

his arm and he stopped talking. They reached the door. Someone had opened it wide. They went outside with Struve, and Bishop shut the door behind them. To his surprise the American relaxed as they took him along to one of the little mezzanines.

"Take your hands off. I won't pull anything."

They let him go. He began rubbing the inside of his left arm where it had been paralyzed. The three of them stood by a small bay window. There was a coffee table and three or four chairs. Bishop thought Struve might be intending to talk to them until the nerves came alive again in his arm, and then swing the table at them.

"Why did you two interfere like that?" His voice was unemotional and steady.

Feurte nodded to Bishop. He'd spent most of his life under water, and hadn't learned to talk, and didn't want to. Bishop told Struve:

"You looked like causing a disturbance in there. People who want to do that at parties get thrown out. It's an old custom."

"I came to talk to Melody. It was no business of yours."

Bishop shrugged. "She didn't seem to be very eager. She asked for help. What would you have done, if you'd been in our position?"

Sweat shone on Struve's face. He had gone

very quiet-eyed. He asked in a dull monotone:

"And what is your position?"

"I'm her escort."

Struve looked at Feurte.

"What about you?"

Feurte said: "I cannot see anything to discuss. A lady was being annoyed, and we did not want a fight at the party. I am surprised the situation was not clear to you."

"So you're surprised. I take a plane over here to see my fiancée, and get hustled out of her party by two muscle men—"

"You are engaged to the lady?" Feurte asked.

"Sure."

"She did not mention that to me. She did not seem to"—he searched for the right word—"be enjoying that relationship, when she asked you to stop annoying her. So I think you are lying."

Feurte looked at him innocently. Struve's jaw line had tightened. Feurte added:

"In any case she has honored me by accepting my invitation to entertain her during her stay in this town. I have a chalet, higher on the hill." He looked at Bishop. Bishop said:

"That's correct."

Struve hit Feurte square on the point of the jaw and Feurte was rocked back as his legs doubled against the edge of the coffee table. Bishop was sizing up when Feurte called:

"No!"

He got his balance and came at Struve. Bishop moved a little to his left and pressed the bell push in the wall. While Struve was in the hotel there would be trouble, and it would make things awkward.

Feurte locked him as Struve brought a knee up. The table went over and began rolling down the three steps of the mezzanine. Bishop picked it up and put it clear of the two men as they lurched suddenly towards the bay window. It had a low sill and Struve had his back to it. As Feurte turned he was knocked sideways and some glass smashed, bits of it tinkling down outside. Feurte was going through, his spine trapped on the edge of the sill. When his legs swung up, one foot kicked at Struve, but Struve was pitching off his balance now.

Some people were opening doors along the passage below the mezzanine, and Bishop saw Melody coming out of the room where the party was. Others were with her. Two of the hotel staff were hurrying up the stairs. They were both big men and it seemed as if someone had phoned for them after Struve had been taken out of the room.

Struve and Feurte had gone through the window. It was on the first floor so Bishop left them and went up to Melody.

"Let's go back and get on with the party," he said.

She stood looking past him to the smashed window, and he knew suddenly from her expression why she had seemed to act out-of-character just now. She was happy. Two men had smashed through a window, fighting over her. The compliment pleased her. From Miss Gorringe, Bishop had learned about the incident that had got her thrown out of her show in London, about the manslaughter case at the Black Orchid. This was another of its kind.

He murmured: "You could have handled Struve yourself, couldn't you, just by telling him where he stood?"

She smiled. Her eyes were bright.

"Of course."

"But it was more fun to promote this fight."

Her smile went. "It's a good idea for men to fight for their women, Hugo. These days we're too often bought with a check." She had to speak more loudly above the babble of excitement in the crowded mezzanine. "Besides, Everett shouldn't have followed me here. It'll teach him to behave."

Bishop watched her face. It was flushed and

alive, and the flecked pale eyes had lost their coldness for a moment. In these few minutes he knew she was happy. There were men in danger, in her name. Perhaps she had been as happy as this only a few times before, during the incident at her show, the other one at the Black Orchid, and others he hadn't heard about. And the night Brain had smashed up?

Struve and Feurte had gone through the window. It was just another incident. But one of them might have hit his skull, might have snapped his spine going over the sill, broken his neck hitting the ground below.

Bishop was alone with her at the fringe of the crowd. The people were enjoying the diversion, as if it had been arranged as an impromptu cabaret for their benefit. Most of them held glasses, and a man was offering odds of two-to-one against the American.

Bishop asked Melody: "Remember the night club where the manager was killed?"

She stared at him, then looked away, saying nothing.

"I expect you do," he said. "And you remember what happened to David Brain. If one of these two has broken his neck falling out of that window, it'll make a third death in your life. Have there been many others, or did you lose the score before you were twenty-one?"

She watched the broken window. It seemed to fascinate her. She didn't answer him. In a minute she suddenly turned and went back into the room. He followed. The records had finished. She lifted some new ones on to the spindle and set the arm. Music came. She turned away from the cabinet and stood against him, saying:

"During the interval there will be dancing."

He began moving with her to the music. Their feet were slow on the soft carpet. As they turned they saw de Whett leaning in the doorway, a drink in his hand. He was smiling gently. Through the music he called:

"Darling, you'll never change. You'll never get tired of things like this. When everything's over, Melody lingers on."

She smiled back; they danced close to him.

"Geoffrey, you're lit, but no one would know. Go and get them back, it's early yet. My party's hardly begun."

12th
MOVE

THE ROOM was quiet. The moon had moved round the sky and there was only a faint splash of its light near the windows. It shone on Melody's sandal. In the corner, one small table lamp burned. Its light was warm, sending a flush across the quiet ceiling. The echo of voices had gone.

The crimson glass ash trays were full. Cigarette ends had fallen into them, scattering ash. The air was stale with their smell. A glass had been broken on the floor near the radio. Another was in fragments by the open French doors. Someone had left a stole; it was draped over the arm of a chair. Pieces of a phonograph record were heaped in a bowl on one of the little tables. The whisky that had spilled from Struve's glass was a damp, oval shadow on the white carpet.

Melody lay on the floor, her head cupped in her raised arms, her arms propped against a cushion that had slipped from a chair. Below the white sheath of her dress, her feet were bare. One sandal was in the cool of moonlight, the other was by the door. She had kicked them off when the last guest had gone.

In the stillness she said: "I want you."

Her voice was soft and rough. The words came slackly from her lazy mouth. She was serious-drunk, the stage when the laughter sticks in the throat and reminiscing starts, with a false, shy, sentimental gravity.

Bishop murmured: "We've been over all that."

He was cradled sideways in a chair, his legs hooked over one of his arms, his shoulders resting against the other. His head was half-turned to look at her. In her white dress she seemed like a faint stream of moonlight across the floor.

"Hugo, one day I'm going to take you."

"For granted?"

"For fun."

He eased himself lower in the chair. The ticking of his own watch was audible. He looked down at it. It was nearly four. He looked above Melody to the windows. The horizon of the sea had more light than the moon's.

"It's morning," he said.

For minutes she was quiet, then: "Please give me a cigarette."

He levered himself out of the chair and sat on his haunches beside her, getting his cigarette case. She didn't move. When he lit a cigarette for her she parted her lips to take it.

In a little while he said: "Enjoy your party?"

"Yes. Did you?"

"Very much." The smoke curled up from her mouth. He watched it. "Don't you want to know how Dominic is?"

"Not especially. He's alive."

"Yes. A bit disappointing for you. Still, even the best parties don't always come off."

"I don't want him dead."

"What about Struve?"

"Everett's a fool. They'll probably charge him. How does the wording go?"

"In England, grievous bodily harm. I don't know how they put it over here."

"Well, he'll get out, I expect. Everett's quick to catch. He doesn't like the law, anywhere."

"Because of the F.B.I. inquiry?"

She watched him steadily, becoming sober slowly.

"Did he tell you about that?"

"No. Why should he? It's not the kind of thing to

throw into light conversation. Not that any conversation I've had with him has been very light."

"You know a lot about people, don't you?"

"An F.B.I. inquiry isn't easily hushed up."

"I don't believe anything could be easily hushed up when you're interested in it."

They stopped talking for minutes. He broke the stillness.

"Tonight I saw how happy it made you, to see men brawling on your account. Reminded me of Diamond Lil."

"Or any woman. Any real woman."

"I've known a lot of real ones. They didn't make a habit of starting slaughter to relieve their ennui."

"Possibly they've no ennui. I've got lots, Hugo. I've had it ever since I found out what men were like."

"And what are they like?"

"A record, stuck in a groove. After a while I went mad listening. Now I smash them, and the music stops."

He said: "And that's your kick out of living?"

"Yes."

"It's a bit negative, isn't it? Going through life switching music off—"

"No, Hugo." Her voice cut across his with sudden soft fierceness, like a cat's paw darting out.

"It's very positive. And I can't do anything else, anything better, anything worse. I'm caught in a jamb and all I can do is kick—"

"What jamb?"

"Myself. Men come for me. Something in my eyes blinds theirs to everything else. But once I've given in, they go. Their senses come back and I don't see them again. Whether I like them a lot or only a little, I can't keep them, once they've known me. I haven't any say. There's nothing I can do."

Bishop stretched his legs out and propped himself on his elbows, watching the flush of light strengthening in the windows. The quietness was as fragile as the faint light of the dawn; it seemed a shout would shatter both.

"How much are you lying to yourself, Melody?"

"Not at all. What would be the point?"

"I don't know, but there could be a very good reason. It's not so easy to believe that a woman like you can be lonely and lost—"

"I'm lonely, but not lost. I know where I am. That's the hell of it. I've got a kind of magnetism that's on an alternating circuit. It attracts and then repels; and it repels for good—"

"I don't believe that."

She leaned forward suddenly.

"Hugo, listen. When I was a kid of seventeen I had all the seventeen-year-old dreams in my head—all the straight conventional ideas about young love and growing into womanhood and meeting someone I could fall in love with for life. Up to a point, it came true. Long before I was twenty I'd had a several affairs; all I had to do was to look at a man I wanted, and he came; we had fun for a few days of a few weeks, and he went. That was all right, because we were young and a marriage with any one of them wouldn't have lasted. Then I met someone I wanted for life. He said the same as the others had said—there was nothing he wouldn't do for me, he'd put the world at my feet, he could never love anyone else. I was deliriously happy. We went to Italy together and came back to England to be married."

She gave him her half-burned cigarette; he reached over to one of the ash trays and pressed it out. She said:

"He left me, just as the others had done, and I couldn't get him back."

Bishop said quietly, "And at the age you were then, it was the end of the world?"

"Yes, Hugo. Until I came to realize the world was round, and didn't have an end. I went round with it again, and before long I knew that for the rest of my life I'd be doing just that. Circling. I didn't fool myself anymore. I just watched it happening to me: another man, and when he'd gone, another man. I was a record, too, stuck in a groove. They wanted me, and if I wanted them I let them take me, and then they drifted away, as if I'd suddenly grown old, or ugly. Sometimes I wondered if it happened because they'd caught sight of the real me, under the veil they'd torn their way through. But inside, I never thought I was old, or very ugly."

She leaned back, as if she were suddenly tired. "At my shining best, I think I'm just plain dull to them, after their fever's gone."

"You really believe that?"

"What else can I believe?"

He didn't answer. Minutes of silence passed before he said gently:

"So you began hating them. Men."

"Yes."

"I suppose that's understandable. But you're still young. If it takes you another ten years to find a man who wants you for life, you won't be starting late—"

"There aren't any men like that. Or I've nothing to offer, except lust for lust. It won't happen, I've known it for a long time now. I'm conditioned, already, to the kind of life that I was born for. I'd be a fool to try changing it." Her voice became low, and the heat went out of it. "Besides, what kind of time would a man have, mated to me? I can't switch off this current of mine that burns men up—God, how I wish I could! A man likes his wife to be admired, but not craved, wherever she goes. And how strong am I? Suppose I couldn't be faithful to one man, after knowing so many? If anyone took me for life, Hugo, he'd be taking poison."

In a moment he said: "So you're just going on?"

"Yes, and I don't mind, now."

"What's happened, to break the strain?"

She looked at him steadily and said:

"I've known David. He's mine for life."

"That's why you talked in the past, when you came to see me in London. Brain was the last of the men, in a way. You don't want any more like him, for life."

"There aren't any more like him, Hugo."

"Out of a few thousand million?"

She smiled slowly. "No two finger prints in the world are the same. And a finger print isn't very complex. People are."

He said carefully: "You intended to have Brain, whatever happened?"

Her voice went cold.

"That's too interrogative."

"You told me that if I came here with you, you'd tell me about him."

"I didn't imagine you'd need telling, and I think I was right. You're doing fine. When you checked the book downstairs, you found his name. This evening when you came to my room, you saw his photograph by my bed. Even when you saw me at Romero's, the night after the crash, you didn't really believe I was there alone. Did you?"

"No, I didn't. When we danced, I felt you were dancing with him, not me."

"I was, until you lost the step."

"That was deliberate," he said. "I didn't like the feeling of being in a haunted ballroom, playing the ghost."

"But you don't mind doing it now?"

"I keep my mind off it."

"You're keeping your side of the bargain. You told me why you were coming here: to find out about David. I asked you to come here to *be* him, in a way. With you, I'm nearer him, because you're the link. And in this place, where he and I were closer than anywhere else, he's nearer still."

"I've changed my identity again, from a ghost to an Indian guide."

"I don't feel anything spiritualistic about David."

"Just plain unhealthy morbid."

"If you will."

He said: "If I'd come to find you in your room today, it would have been like dancing again at Romero's—wouldn't it? I wouldn't have been there."

She got up slowly, lithely, and for a little time stood looking down at him.

"Hugo, don't leave me, will you, for a while?"

"I'm going back in a couple of days."

"That's all right. I'll come too. All I want is to see you sometimes, talk to you. Whatever you call this thing that's going on in my mind—morbidity, sentiment, self-deception—you seem to be able to absorb all of it without getting impatient or contemptuous. That makes me feel all right. I'll get over it. Don't go right away from me until I have."

He stood up. Without thinking, they moved to the French doors. The air was cooler, creeping in from the veranda, brushing their faces.

"I won't," he said, "unless I have to."

She touched his hand. It was a simple movement, thanking him; but he turned away as soon as he could and went slowly towards the door. His hand was his own, not Brain's.

184

He said: "It was a nice party."

"Are you going now?"

"If you don't mind, yes."

The white of her dress glowed softly between the French doors. Morning light was brighter now than the moon's. She looked slim and cool, standing there with one bare shoulder against the doors, her head half-turned to watch him. He murmured:

"You look very lovely."

"Thank you, darling. I know you meant that."

He opened the door.

"See you at breakfast?" he asked softly.

"Yes. On my balcony." He could just make out her smile, in the faint light. "Without obligation."

He closed the door quietly behind him. On the little mezzanine, they had cleared up the few slivers of glass that had fallen inwards, on to the carpet. He walked on, taking the main stairs to the third floor.

He went into his room and turned on the light. Struve didn't make any movement, in the chair. He was just sitting looking at the door.

Bishop closed it and said: "Hello."

"I hope you don't mind my busting in here."

"Not at all."

He came further into the room and stopped, holding out his cigarette case. With his right hand the American reached out and took a cigarette. His left arm was in a sling. Bishop gave him a light and said:

"They tell me Dominic Feurte's going to live. I telephoned about half an hour ago."

"Fine." He drew on the cigarette. "I liked him."

Bishop cocked an eyebrow.

"You did? What d'you do with the people you don't like?"

Struve smiled tightly.

"It was just one of those things. Women are like war. You jump all over your own brother, when he's done nothing at all to you."

Bishop studied him. "Apart from the broken arm and the grazed skull, what's your score?"

"That's the limit. I was lucky. The other guy— what was his name again?"

"Dominic Feurte."

"He fell across a garden seat. I hit the grass clean."

"M'm. Does anyone know you're here in my room?"

Struve shook his head. Bishop looked at the open windows. He said: "We won't talk too loudly. I imagine the police would like to know where to pick you up."

"Why should you worry?"

"Because I want to know you better. I think you

can give me some help." He sat down near the American, crossing his legs.

"What makes you think I'd help you, Bishop?"

"A touching faith in the power of getting a man to talk by giving him what he wants first. What is it you want?"

"Nothing."

"You came here to wait for me. For all you knew I'd turn you straight over to the police on sight. You nearly killed a man, and they think that's a serious thing to do. They'd also ask a lot of questions—you know, who you are and where you come from. And there's a thing or two that you don't particularly want found out. Or should I say raked up? But you risked coming here, so your reason's important. Let's not waste any time—it's daylight again."

"You work everything out, don't you?"

"It keeps me too busy to chalk on walls. What d'you want, Struve?"

The man's face tightened a fraction.

"Just to tell you something. Keep away from Melody."

"Is that all?"

"It's all I want from you."

Bishop got up slowly and began walking about. He said over his shoulder:

"You can't have it. Sorry to be so unaccommodating." He turned. "What else can't I do for you?"

Struve's eyes had gone dull but they didn't waver.

"All right. We know where we stand."

"Now Struve, don't be silly. You can't just walk in here and tell me what you want me to do with my private life." His voice was level, almost friendly. "I don't care a damn who you are, and from the little I've seen of you up to now I've reached the conclusion that the less I see of you again the more wholesome I shall feel. Don't think me unkind, but I regard you as a bad smell, after the manners you showed at the party. There's an ash tray on the table there, by your right arm."

Struve tapped the ash off his cigarette without looking away from Bishop's face.

"You don't pull your punches, do you—"

"Don't tell me you're sensitive."

Struve watched him for a minute without speaking. When he spoke he seemed to have worked something out.

"Exactly where do you come into this, Bishop?"

"This?"

"A guy's just killed himself, driving too fast. You take up with his girl, right away. Why?"

"She's attractive. Don't you think so?"

"It seems I do. She happens to belong to me."

Bishop began moving about again, turning his back on Struve to give him time to get out a gun if he wanted to. He didn't think he had come here without one, because of his arm; and he wasn't here just to smoke a cigarette and tell him to keep away from Melody.

He said: "Now there you go again, Struve. Melody doesn't 'belong' to you. In fact I don't really think she likes you, much. Can't you get these ideas of yours a bit more straight, before you say them aloud?"

He turned round, leaning with his back to the open windows. There wasn't anything in Struve's hand, except the cigarette.

The voice was tight-throated.

"Bishop, you're very smooth. I can be that way, too. I haven't got such a glossy line of spiel, but you'll have to overlook that. I missed college. But I haven't got a head full of loose marbles. What made you so interested in Melody, when Brain killed himself? You'd never met her before. I've checked on that. You've met her a hell of a lot since. Why?"

"So you've got things worked out, too? I'm glad. But has Melody? Or is she a little bit in the dark?"

"About what?"

"Oh, various minor details. For example, you told her you flew into England a couple of days before the inquest on Brian. As a fact, you arrived on the day he crashed."

Struve's face didn't change. He just looked at his cigarette, then looked back, steady-eyed. But it was enough.

Bishop asked: "Does she know that? Were you lying to her, or did she lie to me? It's all rather complicated, isn't it?"

"What's your tie-up, Bishop? You're not official, I know that."

"Of course you do. You wouldn't have come within a mile of me if I were connected with the police or with British Intelligence. They don't like small boys who play with chemicals."

"Just what does that mean?"

"That you're in a spot, wherever you go. You've done too many things on a big scale not to be taken notice of. All the time you toe the line, you're in the clear. But if you do anything to upset the police, they're liable to react. In your country I think it's called putting on the heat."

Struve watched his face, his own blanked. The room was brighter now. The moon had faded out of the sky and the sun was climbing through a thicket of white cloud, over the sea in the east.

"Bishop, the more you talk, the less I think you know."

"Yes?"

Bishop leaned away from the window sill, and moved towards the ivory telephone on the bedside table. He put his hand over the receiver and without looking at Struve said:

"Then I'll talk to someone else, instead."

He lifted the receiver. When the switchboard answered he said quietly in French: "Police, please."

From his chair Struve heard the faint acknowledgment of the voice in the earpiece.

"Bishop."

Bishop looked at him.

"Yes?"

"Tell them to cancel that."

Struve's cigarette was smouldering in the ash tray. He had put it there in order to free his good hand. Even from where he stood, Bishop could see that the safety catch was off.

He dipped the contact a few times and said:

"Switchboard. Please cancel that. It was a mistake."

When he put the receiver down Struve said:

"Now lift your hands and—"

The telephone had traveled about half the distance from the little table to Struve's right hand when he fired. A chip of white plastic flew off it and hit the ceiling before the base caught Struve's right wrist. The wires of the telephone had pulled clean out of their plug socket. The gun went off again when Bishop moved towards the armchair but Struve's wrist had been hurt and the bullet slapped into the curtain pelmet. The telephone had fallen on to the floor and got kicked sideways as Struve jerked his foot up and tried for the groin. He hadn't had any time to get out of the chair yet. Bishop trapped the leg and jerked it by the ankle. Struve's face was dark with pain. When the gun fell, Bishop picked it up and put it on to the bedside table, then helped Struve back into the chair.

He sat like a sack, looking at Bishop, his face slowly whitening, his eyes dull. Bishop took a cigarette out and put it into his lips, lighting it for him.

"I'm sorry, but it was your fault."

Struve said one or two things to him and then Bishop stopped him.

"You shouldn't wave guns about. It makes people jumpy. Now shut up and sit still."

He drew a stool over from the corner, and sat on it facing Struve. He said:

"I want to know something. Just after the war you had an accident in a car. You were driving. How did that accident happen?"

13th

MOVE

♟ MISS GORRINGE got out of the grey Rolls-Royce as Bishop came over from the Customs building. Standing against the limousine she looked cool and elegant in white linen. He said:

"You look like one of our more distinguished duchesses, Gorry."

She smiled. It was good to see him back, even after these few days.

"Thank you, Hugo. Nice time?"

He dropped his bags into the back of the car and they climbed in. The sun was warm on the roof.

"So-so. Nothing much happened, but I've got something to work on at last."

"It was worth going?"

193

"Yes." He started the engine and swung the car out of the enclosure. While they made for West London he told her what had happened in Monte Carlo, and for a time she just sat silently, thinking over the scene. Then she asked:

"And where is Struve now?"

He smiled. "Still there, I imagine. Someone at the hotel knew his name, and gave it to the police after the fight; so he won't be able to show his passport on his way out."

"Then what will he do?"

"He's probably got friends who can help him. He can't stay there, and anyhow he'll follow Melody over here."

"He's really involved with her?"

"No, but he desperately wants to be. I think we can count on him getting here as fast as he can, once she's back herself."

They drove through Bayswater and kept south through the park. Vera Gorringe said:

"How long is she staying over there?"

"Another day. Feurte's out of danger, but she feels a bit responsible about him. I left her talking to him at the hospital." The engine's whisper was the only sound for minutes; then he asked: "What's happened this end?"

"It's been dull, but I've a good deal of background ready for you. Nothing much more about

Everett Struve, I'm afraid."

"He's not the type to leave a very traceable trail, but I've got to know the cause of his car smash in the States. After I'd taken his gun away I pumped him for an hour. Not a word, of any use. He just seized up solid."

She said: "So do his records. I even rang up Freddie, and did a little beating about this particular bush, but he wouldn't play."

"Why not?"

"I don't know. He just dodged it by saying he'd be glad to see you when you got back to London. That was all I could prize out of him."

The car moved slowly into Sloane Square. Bishop said:

"What's he want to see me about?"

"He didn't say."

"Was it just to hedge you off about Struve, d'you think?"

"No, he's quite serious."

"That's interesting. When Freddie asks to see me it means he's excited about something." He spun the big wheel and nosed the ancient limousine southwards from King's Road. "Did he sound excited?"

Miss Gorringe said: "Yes, a little. You know Freddie—when he gets worked up he raises his voice to a quiet grunt."

"I'll phone the old devil."

The tires ran from the smooth macadam on to cobbles; the windshield sent a flash of reflected sunshine across the many-colored doors and window boxes of Cheyne Mews, and the murmur of the engine died away.

"Welcome home."

"Thank you, Gorry."

Bishop phoned the Yard immediately after lunch.

"Inspector Frisnay, please. Mr. Bishop here."

He watched Chu Yi-Hsin while he waited. She watched him back, perched on the corner of his desk, with the tip of her tail just moving.

Vera Gorringe was on the davenport, going through a file of cuttings. She and the Siamese heard the faint voice from the receiver speaking a name they knew.

"Hugo?"

"Hello Freddie, how are you?"

"All right. You?"

"Yes, fine. Gorry said I should ring you."

"I'm glad you did. How busy are you?"

"Not very, for an hour."

Frisnay said: "Can you come round?"

"Is it urgent?"

"It might be."

Bishop looked patiently at the cat on his desk.

"You're just a mine of information, Freddie. Just give me a key word to make me interested."

"Brain."

Bishop said: "I'll be round. 'Bye." He hung up.

Miss Gorringe said: "What was the key word?"

"Brain. Did you tell him we were working on that?"

"Not with so much as one syllable."

Bishop smiled slowly, filling his meerschaum from the tobacco bowl. "Well, he knew how to get me round there."

"You're going now?"

"Yes." He thought for a minute. "That's odd, Gorry, when you come to look at it. I know I was the only eyewitness to Brain's crash, but the coroner's verdict was accidental death. Why should Freddie think I'm still interested in the thing?"

"I could offer you a few theories, Hugo. Freddie can give you a direct answer. Shall I stay here?"

"Unless you want to go out specially."

"No."

"Good. If little Sophie Marsham phones, I'd like to see her. Dinner tonight, if she likes."

"I'll arrange something. She rang while you

197

were away; I said you'd be back this morning."

"Did she say what she wanted?"

"No, but she wasn't particularly evasive either. Just a friendly call, I'd say."

Bishop went down the long room to the door, leaving a faint trail of smoke from his pipe. He said: "If it was just that, it'll be the first instance of simple friendliness anyone's shown since Brain died. All his acquaintances are sitting about the place like cats waiting to spring, though they don't seem to know on whom."

"Could it be you?"

"Can't say, but Freddie might tell me."

He closed the door.

Frisnay was standing at his window. Nobody else was in the office. He turned his head.

"Have a chair," he said. He looked back through the open window. "Between roughly three-five and three-six P.M. in August, the sun manages to send a one-inch beam down between those chimneys up there. So I stand here on a telephone directory with my neck bent double, and sun-bathe, every day. That's how I got this Monte Carlo tan."

Bishop sat on one haunch, at the end of Frisnay's desk.

"Raspberries to you too, little brother," he said.

Frisnay came and sat down in the chair behind his desk and looked at Bishop steadily. He had been born with a long face and level eyes that had a way of staring at people, and when they stared, the people could see all of their past reflected in them. It was most uncomfortable. Bishop didn't mind. He and Frisnay had been staring each other out since their school days in the Upper Fourth.

Frisnay said: "I'm not going to waste your time by pretending I don't know that you've had your big ear to the ground ever since David Arthur Brain was killed."

"You mean you don't want me to waste your time by denying it."

"Yes. Because I think we can help each other."

"I'll do what I can. But you open the batting."

Frisnay stared at him for a full minute and then said: "I've been ordered to investigate a coincidence. Everett Struve, an American citizen, has been watched for some years now in the States. He was concerned in a bad smell, once, on an international scale, and although he was officially exonerated, the F.B.I. haven't dropped the question. If Struve was really guilty of doing a deal with an enemy country during a war, he might do it again if there's another one."

"He sold chemicals, didn't he?"

Frisnay moved his narrow head an inch, but not his eyes.

"I suppose Gorry found that one in her files."

"You'd be surprised, the things she finds there."

"I'm not certain I would. And what has she found out about Brain?"

"A few things. But you were to open the batting."

"All right. From what we know here, Brain wasn't mixed up in Struve's deal. But he was in a position to know about it. For reasons of his own we think he kept quiet."

"Which left him with a hold on Struve?"

Frisnay inclined his head again and stared at Bishop's tie. "I wouldn't call it a hold, except in that he could use it as an influence to keep Struve away from him. They didn't like each other very much, and if Struve started showing up too often in Brain's territory, he was thrown out—by that influence."

Bishop thought for a few seconds. Through the open window came the sound of starlings on the roofs across the yard. He said slowly:

"But all the time Brain had this influence over Struve, Struve couldn't consider himself safe?"

"We think that is so. Brain was a danger to him, an unexploded bomb that could go up at any time, or never." He gave a slight shrug. "This is strictly off the record, Hugo: the coroner says Brain died by accident. But he died on the day when Struve landed here from the States, with a false passport and a motive for murder. That is the coincidence I've been told to investigate."

Bishop said evenly:

"Coincidences happen."

"So does murder."

"Coming from you, Freddie, that sounds a random shot. You really believe Struve murdered Brain?"

"That's my chief theory. Of course I'm going on more than mere coincidence. Dozens of other people arrived in this country the day he died."

"Well, the point's this. Where was Struve at midnight on that date?"

"Quite. We don't know. Do you?"

Bishop shook his head. Ash fell from his pipe on to the desk. Frisnay patiently cupped his hands and blew it clear of his blotter. Bishop said:

"No, I don't. If I did, I'd tell you. No reason why I shouldn't. But I'll tell you other things you might not know. One is that Struve had a car accident just after the war. He was driving. Nobody was with him. He went into hospital for some weeks."

The silence began lengthening. Frisnay asked: "Well?"

"I've a chief theory, too. The same one: Struve somehow killed Brain. But I see a different motive. I knew he was mixed up in this. F.B.I. inquiry, but I didn't know Brain had anything on him. I thought it was the woman who provided the motive."

"Melody Carr."

"Yes. Have you met her?"

"No. You've just left her in France, haven't you? And Struve?"

"Both, yes. As far as I know, she'll be back tomorrow. When Struve will manage to cross the Channel I can't say. He daren't show his passport—"

"We've arranged about that," said Frisnay.

Bishop said: "Really? What sort of arrangement—is he being pulled in?"

"No, let out. Of France. We're doing it through Interpol. Scotland Yard and the F.B.I. want to keep tabs on this man, so it'll be easier when he's back in one of these two countries. The Sûreté isn't so interested, and they've agreed to send him home—"

"To the States?"

"There or here. He's got homes in both places."

"How are the French police arranging this?"

"They're simply telling him to clear out before they charge him with assault—"

"Of Dominic Feurte?"

"Yes."

Bishop swung his haunch off the desk and sat down in one of the leather chairs.

"You've been watching Struve. Don't you know where he went after he landed here ten days ago?"

"We do not. He dived for cover immediately he left the airport. He was picked up the day before the inquest."

"Where?"

"He was seen driving up to the block of flats where the Carr woman lives."

"Does he know he's being shadowed?"

"He may do, or his going to earth might have been a mere precaution—"

"Because he was over here to get Brain?"

Frisnay spread his hands and said nothing.

Bishop said: "Why haven't you talked to Melody Carr?"

"We don't want to talk to anyone, yet. Where d'you think she stands?"

"To lose. She's a psychopath."

"In what way?"

"Persecution complex, if you can give a label to anything as involved as her psychological condition. She's also a nymphomaniac, an egomaniac and practically a necrophile."

"Quite a girl."

"Yes. You know, Freddie, I made the mistake of jumping to the conclusion that in some way she was almost directly responsible for that crash. I might be right, but just now I'm taking it less for granted. When a woman like that is found at the scene of a fatality, conclusions come too easily."

"But you're not ruling her out?"

"No. Are you?"

"We're ruling nobody out."

"What about this ex-convict?"

"Her manager, as was? We've checked up on him and we're satisfied. He was in Ireland when Brain died."

Bishop got out of the chair and walked about. Frisnay watched him.

"Freddie, Brain died bankrupt. Who did that to him?"

"A man called Pollinger."

"Ah."

"You know him?"

"I've met him, at Beggar's Roost. How much did Brain owe him?"

"Pollinger sued him for seven thousand, about a year ago."

"What sort of debt was it?"

"Private."

Bishop wanted to mention the gaming room that Gorry had found clinging to her private grape vine; but her information hadn't been checked on. In any case, Brain couldn't have lost the seven thousand to Pollinger on the roulette wheel. If Pollinger sued for losses, he'd finish in prison.

Frisnay said: "Just now you said something about a car accident that Struve had. Why does it worry you?"

"It doesn't worry me. I'm just interested. Gorry can't find out what caused the crash. It might have been drink, as with Brain: but was it drink that killed Brain?"

"You feel there's a connection between the two crashes?"

For some time Bishop didn't answer. Frisnay waited. A telephone rang before Bishop spoke.

The receiver came off. "Yes?"

Vaguely his voice reached Bishop's mind as he thought about the two car smashes. When he surfaced, he heard Frisnay saying into the telephone:

"Struve. Ask Tulley if he can find out anything

about an accident he had in the States just after the war." He glanced at Bishop and cupped the mouthpiece. "Can we phone Miss Gorringe and get a more detailed fix?"

"I should think so."

Frisnay talked into the telephone again and then hung up. Bishop said:

"Have they still got the wreck of Brain's Ventura at East Knoll?"

"Yes. We've asked them not to touch it again until we give them the all-clear."

"Why, Freddie?"

"Something might come up, and we might want to look at it again." He waited for what was in Bishop's mind.

"Now listen, *mon vieux*. You can follow this up or tell me I'm a sucker for fairy tales. I don't mind what you do about it. These are the facts: the Ventura has the kind of hood that's hinged at the back and locked at the front. There are no ventilator louvers either in the hood itself or at the sides where the front fenders join it. There is a metal pan surrounding the crankcase to stop road dirt flying up on to the engine. There are two air vents to cool the front brakes, but they're closely grilled with wire mesh and they don't open into the engine compartment anyway."

Frisnay stared steadily. A telephone rang a-
gain. He moved the switch to engaged. Bishop
said:

"But there's a dead moth under the hood."

He struck a match to relight his tobacco. Frisnay said:

"A moth."

The match end pinged into the metal ash tray
on Frisnay's desk and bounced out on to his fold-
er. He picked it up carefully and put it back.

"It's a biggish moth," said Bishop, "and it was
crushed to death against a hood strut."

Frisnay asked straight away: "How did it get
in there?"

"I've given you the picture, Freddie. You tell
me."

For a few minutes Frisnay doodled a sketch
on his blotter. Then he said:

"Crushed?" He sounded puzzled.

"Yes."

"Badly?"

"Yes. It went in there very fast. I don't know
how fast a moth like that can go, but I don't think
it could make a mess of itself that size by hitting
anything stationary."

There was silence again. The pencil moved
cautiously over the blotter.

"It sounds a weird sort of situation."

"Yes, doesn't it."

"I'm not a mechanic, nor an insectologist."

"Nor am I. But the foreman at the garage couldn't give me the answer, and he's a good mechanic."

Frisnay moved the phone switch and picked up the receiver.

Bishop heard only the rasp of sibilants from the earpiece. Frisnay said: "Who wanted me?" He listened for a minute and then said: "Right, please get me Tulley." Bishop heard a click. "Tulley, consider this query about the car accident that Everett Struve had as priority. If necessary use cables."

As he asked for switchboard again he poked a finger at the auxiliary earpiece. Bishop took it off the hook and held it to his ear. When the East Knoll Garage came through, Frisnay asked to speak to the foreman. There was a minute's delay before he came on.

"Good afternoon. Detective-Inspector Frisnay here—I'd like to put a technical question about that smashed Ventura."

"Right, sir."

Frisnay jerked his level brown eyes at Bishop, feeling slightly foolish as he spoke.

"There's a dead moth under the hood. Can you tell me how it got there?"

They both heard a grunt of amusement from the foreman.

"That's what Mr. Bishop gave me to puzzle out, few days ago. It got me right up a tree."

"It did? And are you still up there?"

"I am, sir. But I expect it's just one of those little things we can never put a name to, see?"

"Ye-es," said Frisnay. "Look here, it *appears* that the moth could only have got in when the hood was raised. Would you say that?"

"Well, yes, I would. There don't seem any other way. Not that size. Gnats, yes. Not that thing, never."

"I see. The car hasn't been touched, has it, since you dragged it in there?"

"No, sir. Your order."

"Good. I appreciate your co-operation. It might be valuable." He jerked his eyes at the clock on the desk. "I'm going to send a couple of men down to you within a few hours. They won't get in your way if you just leave them to look round the car. Is that all right?"

"Certainly. I shall be here, if they want any help."

"That's very good of you, thanks."

"You're welcome, sir."

When Frisnay rang off, Bishop put the auxiliary earpiece back on its hook.

"What are you going to do, Freddie?"

He got another stare.

"Get my head tested."

"For gremlins?"

"For moths." He picked up the telephone again. "The Ventura's going to be pretty dusty by now, but we might still find prints if we're lucky."

"Finger prints? Where?"

"On the hood lock. That's right, isn't it?"

Bishop nodded.

"That's right," he said.

14th
MOVE

MISS GORRINGE sounded pleased.

"You can take me out to tea. At Fortnum's."

Bishop looked at the wreckage of his campaign on the chessboard and got up.

"Proper *coup de grâce*."

"You don't have to sound so surprised, Hugo. It's not the first time I've wiped the board with you." She lit a cigarette, spreading herself comfortably on the davenport and putting her feet up on a stool.

"It's the first time you've done it in half an hour."

"I was inspired. By Scotland Yard. When Scotland Yard telephones me for information from my secret files, I can do almost anything—"

"In an access of smug conceit."

She ignored this. She said: "The little matter of the dead moth amuses me. I picture Freddie with a butterfly net and deerstalker hat, down on his knees after aphides and Red Admirals."

"Well, it was my idea."

"Yes. I've pictured you like that too." Her tone lost its lightness. "How much is there to it, Hugo?"

He shrugged. "You know the facts. If they can get any prints from the hood lock, and they're the ones we want, Freddie might take a chance and grab Struve. But it'd be tricky evidence for the prosecution to handle."

"It's not the only evidence, though."

"That's true. It's Freddie's pigeon. We can leave it to him and concentrate on the rest of the picture."

The telephone rang; he answered it.

"Sophie Marsham," her voice came.

"How are you?"

"Very well. Was it a nice trip?"

"It was interesting. I was hoping you'd phone, so that I could suggest a meeting—"

"I rang for that reason. Would it be possible to see you this evening, here?"

"Where is 'here'?"

"I'm at my flat. I'd like to whip up a modest dinner for two."

Her voice was as delicate as her features, and as clearly defined. She sounded more assured than when he had met her at Beggar's Roost. He hesitated.

"I don't see why you should have to do the cooking. Why don't we go—"

"I would like it. And I can cook."

"I'm sure you can. I'd love to come. What time?"

"Sevenish?"

"I'll look forward to it."

"I shall, too. Good-bye."

He just had time to say good-bye before the line went dead. He put down the receiver and looked at Miss Gorringe.

"Little Sophie is markedly streamlined, Gorry."

"I had the same impression, when she rang me. Brief encounters on the telephone are rather refreshing. And she knows how to say good-bye."

"She can cook, too."

"You're dining at her flat?"

He looked reflectively at his checked King. "Yes. Where is it?"

"Twenty-five Elton Street." She observed him with her quiet, colorless eyes. "Hugo, quiet apart from your doubtful attractions as a male, why does she want to talk to you so urgently?"

"D'you think it's very urgent?"

"She rang when you were away, and again now. I'm certain it's not because she loves the way the dial spins back with that wonderful clicking noise."

He said: "I think you're right. When I met her at the roadhouse I felt she wanted to know something. It appears she didn't find out, so is having another go."

"What do you imagine she wants to know?"

"At first I thought it was my opinion of the inquest. She doesn't agree with it—"

"Did she say so?"

"No. But she doesn't."

Miss Gorringe watched her cigarette for a time and then said quietly: "Is she protecting anyone, do you think?"

"It could be, but who?"

"The dead?"

"Is that just an idea, Gorry?"

"I'm afraid so. I've no evidence."

"M'm. . . . There's no evidence against Everett Struve that you could find in a haystack, but if he had nothing to do with that death I'm a Mongolian manglemonger." He gazed at the Siamese, who was asleep on the top of the piano. "I'll try following that line, this evening. I might learn more about Brain from Sophie than I did from Melody."

"She was really in love with him. Melody wasn't—if one can judge what goes on between one person and another, on that scale."

"Sometimes the people themselves can't really weigh it up."

"I think these can. There's nobody in this case who doesn't know where he or she is going—or where they've been. Brain was a stormy bird who was obviously born for a violent end. Melody is a white-hot hellcat with no heart and a tangled nervous system. Struve is a big-time con artist who's trigger-happy and allegedly traitorous. Sophie is the sort of girl who could take care of herself on a burning ship full of starving lions in a mid-Pacific typhoon. I'm not sure about this Geoffrey de Whett—I've not met him."

"De Whett?" Bishop tilted his chair back until it touched the wall. "I'm not sure about him, either. I had the impression he ran deep. He and Struve knew each other, although neither bothered to mention it. I'd still like to know exactly where de Whett was on the night of Brain's death. He said he wasn't in England, but then he said quite a lot of things I didn't believe—"

"I took the opportunity of doing a little deal with Mr. Tulley of the Yard, when he phoned me about Struve's car crash. I said if he ever found out where de Whett was on that night,

I wouldn't consider the information as entirely unwanted."

"Nice."

"Thank you."

He looked at the time. "You've earned your tea."

The flat in Elton Street was three floors up. The elevator was tiny and short-winded; its cables creaked in constant alarm; but just as Bishop was looking for something in the ceiling to grab at when it fell, it stopped at the third floor with a quiet shudder.

Sophie Marsham was in a house coat, entirely black to contrast with her ash-blonde hair. She stood in the doorway looking smaller than ever, and he remembered Miss Gorringe's succinct summing-up. He felt the girl would have been pleased with that portrait of herself.

They said nothing about Brain until she had piled the plates in the kitchen. It had been a beautiful pilaff; during the meal there had been no feeling of restraint over the table in the dining alcove; a half-bottle of Barsac had relaxed their reserve.

"Sophie, that was superb."

He was sitting in a Knoll chair, half his face in

shadow, his legs stretched out.

"Rather simple, I'm afraid."

"The superb can never be achieved with sophistication. You discovered that long ago."

She came into the tiny room, dropping a cushion on to the floor and perching on it to face him.

"I'm unsophisticated?"

"In that you lack artificiality."

She smiled. "I lack a lot of things."

"But you don't miss them."

"Sometimes. Tell me about Monte Carlo."

He watched the slight poise of her head for a moment before he answered, wondering how much she knew.

"It was interesting, as I told you over the phone. I stayed at the hotel where David used to go."

He was watching her eyes. They changed. Pain came into them and then she smiled again and said quickly:

"Did you?"

He wished he had not been so direct; but it had helped him to get at the truth, and that was why he had said it. Gorry was right: the girl had been in love with David Brain, and probably still was, but in a different way from Melody.

"You must have met some of his friends there," she said lightly. "And some of Melody's—she went with you, your aunt told me."

He paused. "I don't know about friends. There were people who knew them, and remembered David. One of them was a man called Geoffrey de Whett."

"At the Casino—yes?"

Bishop nodded. She said: "He still haunts the place, then. It's rather sad."

"He didn't look especially sad about anything. Not even about meeting his wife again."

"You mean Melody."

He nodded again. "Why does he haunt the Casino?"

She sat curled on the cushion, holding her ankle and watching the glint of a simple gold ring on her left hand. Bishop thought probably Brain had given her that. She wore no other.

"Didn't he tell you? He tells most people. He lost almost everything he possessed, at the tables one night. About five years ago."

"It ruined him?"

She nodded. "Yes, except for a small, permanent income that he couldn't touch. He lives on that, now."

"Why doesn't he start up again?"

She looked at him in silence for a moment, then said:

"There's nothing to start. There never was. He's a typical piece of disintegrating Riviera flotsam. He just sits there in the sunshine taking a delight in watching what he calls 'the old order' falling slowly to pieces, like he's doing himself."

The ring flashed in the light as she moved, reaching for the box of cigarettes on the wall table. She held it out to Bishop and then suddenly remembered:

"You don't smoke cigarettes."

He said: "No, thank you."

She put the box back and stood up, small and straight, with her hands in the pockets of the house coat, her fair hair falling forward a little as she looked down at him.

"This is an odd meeting, Hugo."

"Is it?"

"Yes. We each want to find out what the other knows, don't we? And we're scared to show our hand."

"Not scared, perhaps. Uncertain how to find the common focus—"

"That's David. Isn't it?"

"His death. I speak for myself."

"His death doesn't interest me very much—"

"But you were in love with him."

Simply she said: "Yes, I was in love with him."

"You accept his death, and the way he died?"

"How was that?"

"He was murdered."

She went white, and put a hand out to touch the mantel piece as he stood up quickly, holding her arm. She was staring at him vacantly.

"Come and sit down," he said.

She couldn't look away from him. Her lipstick made a bright gash on her bloodless face.

In a dead voice she murmured: "I'm all right."

Expression came back to her eyes; their stare was no longer vacant. Her mouth even tried a feeble smile.

She said again: "I'm all right." Her arm was warm under his hand; she looked down at it, as if puzzled. He stood back, taking his hand away, and she lifted her head again. Color was creeping back to her face. He said:

"How well do you know Everett Struve?"

For what seemed minutes she didn't answer, didn't look away from his face. Then in a soft, bewildered voice she asked:

"Everett Struve? He's the American?"

"He was at the inquest."

Like a child learning slowly, "That's right. Melody knows him." She looked small and cold and hurt. Her tongue sounded bruised in her mouth. "I don't know him very well, Hugo."

He made her sit down in the chair he had just left.

"Shall I get you a drink?" he asked gently.

She shook her head. "Who was it? Tell me."

Her color was almost normal again, and her voice was strengthening.

"I don't know, Sophie. We've one or two theories—"

" 'We'?"

He sat down on the edge of the low brocade stood, his hands loose in front of him.

"I'm in touch with one or two people who are interested in David's crash."

"Who are you? A plain-clothes man?"

"No."

"I must know who you are." There was no hostility in her voice, nor suspicion. She just wanted to know.

"I'm simply interested in personal crises."

"That's awfully vague."

"I suppose it is. But I saw David die. No one else was there. Yet I don't know how he died, and others do."

"What others?" She leaned forward. Her grey-green eyes were wide, flecked in the lamplight. They were lambent and beautiful.

"Can you suggest who they are?" he said quietly.

"Please tell me. I must know."

"I'm sorry. For one thing I'm not sure myself who they are. And if I were, I couldn't tell you their names. I should merely have to pass them on to the police."

She raised her hands slowly, putting their fingers against her cheeks, pressing them, watching him with a quiet, grave intentness.

"Do the police think he was murdered, Hugo?"

"At the inquest, a verdict was returned. Unless new evidence comes to light, there's no action for the police or anyone else to take—"

"Except you."

"I'm only following a personal theory."

"On new evidence that has come to light?"

"Partly."

She folded her arms, her hands lying flat across her slight shoulders. She didn't glance away from him once.

"Yes, an odd meeting. Each trying to find out what the other knows. And only one of us succeeding. . . . "

He smiled faintly.

"So I've helped you?"

"No. Not with a word. The success is yours—"

"Then why were you shocked when I said David was murdered?"

"Not because I didn't know. It was because you'd found out, too. How did you?"

"By no direct means. By talking to people, looking again at the wreck of the Ventura, adding things together, meeting Melody and Struve and Geoffrey de Whett. And you."

"Yes . . . I'm one of the others, who know how David died, aren't I?"

"On your own admission."

In a slow, matter-of-fact voice she said: "I'm sorry I can't tell you any more."

"Someone will," he said, "sooner or later."

"You'll get it from them with your gentle shock-tactics?"

"Perhaps. But I don't always know when I'm using them, until I see the effect."

"Like two people, coming on each other in the dark."

"It's rather like that."

Silence came, suddenly. They were aware of their nearness to each other, the small intimacy of the room, the soft glow of the lamp, the lack of sounds from other flats, other buildings, the street below. The rest of the world might have been dead, leaving them marooned up here together.

The spell and the silence ended when she began suddenly to talk, quickly and softly, looking away from him at last, looking at nothing here in the room.

"I don't think he was one of the people who knew how he died. I think it was all too quick for him. And he'd been drinking, so it must be right."

"The autopsy confirmed that," he murmured evenly.

"Oh, I don't doubt her word. Melody is honest, as honest as any human being ever is. So was David. But there's a lot more to honesty than mere truthfulness—there's directness, cruelty, a disregard for people's hurts. And David was honest with himself, and hurt himself more than anyone else."

Bishop said deliberately: "He didn't strike me as having been a hypersensitive type—"

"No, he wasn't." Her defense of him was quick. "But he wasn't inhuman. He didn't drink heavily just for the kick he got out of it."

Bishop waited. The rose-shaded lamp cast the shadow of her hair against her brow, of her lashes against her cheeks; it glinted across the crimson nail lacquer, burned on the thin gold ring, touched softly the outline of her breasts as she leaned forward in the chair. The young, exquisite face looked suddenly older as she said slowly:

"He drank because it helped him forget. In the war he flew bombers. The night when he led his squadron on a sortie over Belgium, they met trouble. They were caught suddenly in a blaze of light from the ground—a searchlight base that was never suspected in that area had thrown up every beam it had. The planes might have been flying in broad daylight, for all the cover they had. Most men would have turned back while there was time."

She got up suddenly and leaned with one shoulder against the window frame. Her voice lost strength, sounding out softly through the open window, no longer trapped by the walls.

"When he talked to me about it, afterwards, he always put it down to sheer bloody-mindedness. That was his phrase for it. Whatever made him go on, it can't affect the outcome. They were in a straight course, dead in line with their objective, and they reached it within five or six minutes. But by that time they were flying in the middle of a barrage from ground guns that was inescapable. He said there was as much explosive going down as there was coming up. Their objective was wiped out within two minutes; the squadron was wiped out soon afterwards, except for the leader. He came down on fire. There were four survivors out of the sixty men who had left England ninety minutes before."

For the first time the sound of a car's movement rose from the street. It changed gear and droned into a side road, fading on the air. Her head turned as she watched it vanishing.

His voice reached her.

"Was the objective to be bombed at all costs?"

"No. It wasn't a special mission. The squadron leader had the usual right of discretion. He could have used it." She turned suddenly and there was an edge on her voice. "David knew all those men personally. They all liked him. Some of them were his best friends. His own danger was his own choice, but he shouldn't have chosen for them. Hugo, it was a massacre, and there was no justification."

"Did he realize that?"

"Yes. He spent four months in a prison camp before he escaped and reached England. He'd thought it all out, by then. He asked to be put into fighters, and before the war ended he crashed twice, once ramming an enemy plane and bailing out over the sea, the other time hitting a pylon when he was strafing factories on the French coast. The Resistance got him clear. But he never took the responsibility of leadership again. These were solo missions."

She came away from the window, catching a glimpse of her face in the mirror on the wall, then looking away.

Quietly Bishop said: "There's something you've left out. Isn't there?"

She looked down at him, standing still.

"I'm telling you all I can, because I want you to know him better."

"All right, I'll settle for that."

In a moment she said: "After the war he went to see the relatives of the men in the bomber-squadron. He told them exactly what had happened. It was a horrible example of his kind of honesty; he had to confess to them that he'd been solely to blame; if he'd turned his planes back after they'd run into the searchlights they wouldn't have met the barrage; Operations thought the target was only lightly defended— a reasonable risk on a routine sortie. He did his best to explain these things, to convince them that he was responsible for a pointless tragedy. For the sake of his own conscience he told the truth, and didn't care how much it hurt those people to hear it. Some of them were sympathetic, said it couldn't be helped, it was war. Others were less kind; he got back a little of the cruelty he was giving out so generously in the name of honesty."

"Did he expect to be forgiven, by them all?"

"No. He wanted them to know; he was concerned only that he made them see. It didn't matter what he made them feel. It wasn't enough that he killed those men and left their families to believe they'd died most gloriously in action against the enemy. He had to tell them there'd been no need for it, that there was no glory, but only the disciplined obedience of men to a leader they trusted, and who let them down, and let them die."

The phrase sounded odd, coming again softly from her bleak, hurt mouth—"out of sheer bloody-mindedness."

He said: "He meant he was going to bomb the target, at all costs and to hell?"

"Yes. Without resort to reason."

"Wasn't there any inquiry, by the Air Ministry?"

"Yes. The loss of a squadron couldn't be accepted as merely a misfortune of war. But no blame was attached to David."

"Didn't he confess to his action, as he did to the relatives of the men who were killed?"

She smiled; it was just a cold, bright movement of her mouth.

"Yes, he did. But one of the other three survivors had reached England with him. He was one of David's best friends, and he denied that there was any blame to be attached to anyone. It was just bad luck. The authorities felt that David was being too hard on himself, giving himself a guilt complex. It was the first time that anything had appeared in his record to cast doubts on a fine reputation as an officer and a flyer. And they felt that the other pilot would have made any just complaint of irresponsible leadership if there had been any to make, since he was a witness at an official inquiry."

She lowered herself to the floor and held her knees, resting her chin on her clasped hands. "His name was Peter Bridges. I never met him. He must have been a very good person."

"Why do you believe David, and not Bridges?"

"Why would David say that about himself, if it weren't true?" She was puzzled.

Bishop shrugged with his hands.

"I knew a man who gave himself no mercy because he'd failed to rescue his wife when their house caught fire. He did all he could, going in two or three times before the flames drove him back. He couldn't reach her. Afterwards he accused himself of cowardice to all his friends, and said that any man with any guts would have managed to get her to safety. He said he'd never forgive himself."

She watched his face, her eyes still puzzled.

"Why did he do that?"

"Because three months before the fire he'd killed his mistress and buried her in a marsh, and the guilt came out in disguise. He couldn't have lived with it much longer, without confessing his crime. This relieved him of the burden. He'd really tried to rescue his wife—the fireman testified to that."

"He . . . sort of transferred his conscience?"

"Yes. It didn't last him long, because the body of the woman was found by a party of duck shooters, and her death was traced to him. But that was his motive, in reviling himself about the fire."

He thought she had gone a little pale. She was looking away from him now, down at her feet. Quietly she said: "I don't think it was like that with David. He was too straight."

"Human beings are never straight, Sophie. Our minds are spirals, curves, zigzags, circles—because before we can get anything straight in them, something gets in the way: a prejudice, a principle, a fear, a doubt, an inhibition. With most of us, every serious thing that we contend is already conditioned by years of living, of experiencing half-truths and paradoxes and distortions and illusions. We're not to blame. That's life. Most of the time we don't even realize why we do things, and say things."

Resting her brow on her knees so that all he could see was the bright floss of her hair she said: "I'm not certain I understand, or agree."

Steadily he said: "I was in the public gallery

at Number One Court when the man I told you about was tried for murder. He was an unimaginative man, callous and careless. He said—and we believed him—that it hadn't meant very much to him that he'd killed a woman and buried her secretly. It never cost him any sleep, afterwards. He was sorry she had got in his way, but it was her fault, she deserved it. Even at his trial he spoke quite unemotionally about what he had done. He really and honestly believed that he wasn't affected by his murdering. But underneath he was, and it had to come out. It came out after the fire and his wife's death. He didn't know he was using the chance of getting the guilt off his chest; he was quite sincere when he blamed himself for the death of his wife—whose life he'd tried hard to save—instead of for the death of his mistress, whose life he had taken. Psychiatrists call it guilt-transference. I call it making a scapegoat for the conscience. It works in smaller ways, with all of us, every day, and like most emotional motives it goes on underneath—"

"That isn't what happened with David." She spoke into the hollow of her body, her hands tightening round her knees, her face buried. "It isn't what happened with him."

"Why are you certain?"

She raised her head. Her eyes were unnaturally bright. She had been forcing tears back, for minutes.

"I'm just certain," she said.

"Because you've got to be." His voice was hard.

"Why do you say that?"

"I think it's true. Telling me about David, you left something out. But it fits into the pattern I've just built up. And that was your second shock tonight."

She stared at him for a moment and then smiled, as she had smiled before. Nothing of it reached her eyes.

"Anyone would think you were my enemy."

Carefully he said: "Do you?"

She hesitated, then shook her head, and the smile took on a little warmth. "No. But I'd like us to be friends. For tonight, can we forget David?"

"I can." His tone was less hard. "Can you?"

"Oh, yes."

She uncurled her body and stood up. Her scent came to him on the moving air as she passed him and went to a little cabinet by the window. "There's liqueur brandy. Join me?"

He watched her open the doors of the cabinet, with deft, easy movements of her small hands. Her second shock had come only minutes ago, but her poise was perfect again.

"I'd love to," he said, and stood up, still watching her, admiring how steadily she poured the two liqueurs. She was as composed now as she had been when he had come here this evening, as when she had believed there was a certain justice in Brain's death, because of the murdered squadron.

She turned, bringing the glasses.

"What are you thinking, Hugo?"

"I was admiring your perfect poise."

Her smile was easy; it lit the grey-green eyes.

"A girl has to have it," she said, "or fall."

15th

MOVE

THE FORTY-HORSE-POWER engine of the grey Rolls-Royce sent only a soft wash of sound against the buildings as its lights winked back from reflecting surfaces. It turned at Wellington Memorial and moved along Knightsbridge, the tire treads sounding a ceaseless bee-drone over the warm macadam.

The Wolseley picked up on it in a long surge of acceleration and slid alongside. The tingle of its police bell turned Bishop's head. The Wolseley drew forward and slowed, the uniformed observer's hand dipping from the near-side window, signing him to stop.

He checked his speed; it was thirty-five miles per hour. He brought it down to zero. The engines of both cars idled, alongside the pavement.

A man got out of the prowl car and walked back to the Rolls-Royce. Bishop recognized him.

"My dear Frederick, I thought it was a pickup."

Frisnay stood looking down at him through the open driving-window.

"Hello, chum," he said. "I just thought we'd exchange any information, since you're out of your bed. Or are you too busy?"

Faintly from across St. James's they could hear the midnight chime of Big Ben coming.

"I'm not busy," said Bishop. There was something on Frisnay's mind. He was looking bored. "Who's going to drive who, or do we stay here? What's the situation?"

Frisnay said: "I've got to keep moving, and I'd rather do it in my own car. Leave yours here if you like."

Bishop got out and locked up. As he walked with the Inspector towards the black Wolseley they heard a call coming through. The interchange of voices loudened as they got into the back of the car.

Hello P-X-5 . . . hello P-X-5 . . . Message. P-X over.

Hello P-X . . . Go ahead. P-X-5 over.

Report from all-night café at Shoemaker Street—Shoemaker Street—a man resembling Struve left there five minutes ago towards sta-

tion—five minutes ago towards station . . . Ren-
dezvous with P-X-9 . . . See what you can pick up.
P-X over.

Hello P-X . . . Message received. Proceeding to
Shoemaker Street. P-X-5 out.

The call had begun sounding in Knightsbridge.
It ended halfway to Shoemaker Street, a mile
away, for the car began moving north immediately the name of the rendezvous had come over
the air.

The observer turned his head.

He said to Frisnay: "That's three from the
bridge area, sir."

"Yes."

The constable looked at Bishop.

"'Evening, sir."

"Good evening," said Bishop. He looked at Frisnay. "So Struve is back in London?"

"In London, that's all we know."

A call was going out from P-X to P-X-9 again,
repeating the rendezvous with Frisnay's car.
The voices faded for fifty yards as the Wolseley
passed a massive building between its receiver
and base, the short, stiff radio beam blanked by
the mass of stone; then it cleared and strength-
ened. Location of P-X-9 was Molbridge Road.
The Wolseley was moving towards the other
car and the café with thirty seconds more to

go. The man resembling Struve had increased his start to six minutes and a half.

Bishop asked quietly: "When did he get back?"

"This evening. He was taped until he left the airport, then they lost him. He ducked quick."

"Was the woman with him—Melody Carr?"

"Yes. They're watching her flat."

"What's he wanted for?"

"Questioning."

The car slewed into a narrow street and the wheel self-centered smoothly through the driver's hands. A café sign made a glow of light near the other end of the street. A saloon car with aerial antenna was moving in from the north.

The Wolseley's observer took his telephone from its clamp.

Hello P-X . . . Location Shoemaker Street . . . Have joined P-X-9. . . . 5 over.

The static whispered again.

Hello P-X-5 . . . Location received. P-X out.

The two cars slid to a halt outside the café. The observers crossed the pavement and went inside. The drivers waited, engines idling. A call was going out to P-X-10 from base.

Frisnay sat with his hands on his lap.

"We were trailing Struve as routine," he said quietly. "He was allowed to leave the airport without any hindrance. Soon after he ducked and we lost him, we had a message from Monaco. Lifeguards had found a man floating in the harbor with a bullet in his brain. He was about twelve hours dead. That makes the shooting at six A.M."

He stopped talking while a call went out to the G.P. patrol, location three streets distant and moving towards the station. When they signed off he said: "Half an hour later we had identification through. The body was Geoffrey de Whett's."

Bishop thought back. In a moment he said:

"If Struve shot him, he did it within an hour of leaving my room at the hotel."

"He left at about five in the morning?"

"Yes."

Frisnay nodded. "That's why I thought we could usefully exchange information."

The observers came back to their cars.

"All very vague, sir." The door slammed. "Description is roughly correct, but there's nothing definite." He picked up his telephone and began reporting to P-X.

In a moment the car moved off under new orders. Frisnay asked Bishop:

"What happened, between you and Struve when he was in your room?"

Bishop told him briefly. At the end Frisnay asked:

"What became of the gun?"

"He took it away with him."

"You gave it back to him?"

"Yes. I didn't want it, and he was less touchy by the time he left."

"What sort of gun was it?"

"A point-five."

Frisnay looked out of the window as the car turned past the station approach.

"The bullet in de Whett came from a point-five. Where did Struve go, after leaving you?"

"I don't know. He went out of the hotel; I saw him from the window."

"He had a broken left arm?"

"Or fractured. Not in plaster. A sling."

"How much could he use it?"

"Not at all, from the look of it."

"But he might have been shamming?"

"I don't think so. He didn't bring it into play when I threw the telephone at him."

Frisnay was silent for a time. The observer took another call and the Wolseley turned west along Bayswater Road. For two miles there was only the occasional sound of static on the radio and the hum of the transmitter in the back of the car.

"Struve seems a wild boy," Frisnay said ruminatively.

"Almost too wild."

"How d'you mean?"

"If we get his prints from that hood lock, it'll indicate that his methods can be subtle. Why should he go to the trouble of arranging a death in that way—and risk its not coming off—when he's prepared to shoot out of hand?"

"We don't know he shot de Whett—"

"Agreed, but he didn't hesitate to shoot at me. I was just lucky to get off with a chipped telephone."

Frisnay said: "It's a point."

"What about motive, Freddie?"

"I was hoping you'd give us a lead on that. You saw both men there."

The car swung south through gardens, sending location to base. Bishop said slowly: "I didn't see them together. At the party, they didn't talk; there wasn't time; Struve began starting trouble the moment he got inside the room. But I had the impression they knew each other."

"But not affectionately?"

"No. Certainly they must have heard about each other, because de Whett was Melody's husband, and Struve her importunate lover."

"Could be a *crime passionel.*"

"As a snap theory."

They stopped talking to listen to a call going

through from P-X-9 to base.

... Questioned and released. His description could fit Struve, but it was another false alarm. Name: Albert Johns ... Albert Johns ... of 30–three-oh–30 Lexington Way ... a hotel porter. P.X-9 over.

Hello P-X-9 ... report received ... proceed to box factory in Vauxhall Mile ... Carmelite Box Company ... two men seen on premises. ... P-X-9 over.

Acknowledgment went back to base. The car accelerated and turned off by Sloane Square. Frisnay said:

"D'you think Struve might try to get in touch with you now that he's back?"

"Only if I get in his way."

"Are you liable to?"

"Not very, considering he's gone underground. I shall be calling on Melody Carr, but I shan't find him there, if you're watching the place."

Frisnay grunted.

"Well, if you smell him, give us a fix, Hugo."

"I'll do my best."

"Good man. And listen, if we manage to pin de Whett's murder on him, there'll be a trial and you'll be a witness to his movements prior to the alleged act. If you feel like making any notes on what you can remember now, it might keep the evidence nicely on ice. These little things are a help."

"You think there's not much doubt about this?"

"There's always doubt about everything. But if I had to bet on it, I'd put my shirt on Struve—over the rope."

16th
MOVE

SOUTH AMERICAN rhythm beat down from the spot-lit dais, filling the ballroom, ebbing to the walls and to the ceiling and the windows, reverberating and beating back, long rubber ripples of rhythmic sound, surrounding the people. Their limbs were trapped in its tide; they moved with it as if they moved in a current; their feet stamped on the maple floor; their feet laughed whitely; their voices came, emphasizing the relentless beat of the sticks on the taut skin of the drums.

From the dais there came to them the smile of Manuelo. It was one of those smiles that dark-skinned people have, that infect the moods of others with something like sudden personal sunshine. Manuelo's smile was wide and white and sunny; he let everyone see it; it was the goodwill of his business and it earned him more than his music ever would.

There were fifty people in the room, a score at the Bar Copacabaña, a score on the balcony outside, a group of a dozen by the dais. The place had the atmosphere of *fiesta*, and Tom Pollinger was pleased. More people would be coming in soon. It was hours to midnight yet. Business was fine.

"Business looks fine," said Bishop. He was perched at the bar. Pollinger turned and smiled, as sunny as Manuelo.

"It's not bad," he said. "People are happy to-night."

He glanced at the woman who sat next to Bishop. Bishop said: "Gorry—Tom Pollinger. Mr. Pollinger—Miss Gorringe."

She said: "We're happy, too. This is the first time I've come to the Roost. It's better than they say."

He saw that her dress was signed by Dior, and wondered whose widow she was. She looked happy and wealthy. Pollinger liked happy, wealthy people at Beggar's Roost.

He said: "Miss Carr is on her way here. I expect you knew. She phoned me. You've a table booked?"

"Not yet," said Bishop.

Pollinger beamed. "I'll fix it for you."

Bishop stopped him as he turned away.

"Did Miss Carr ask if we were here?"

"Why, yes. When people phone to say they're coming to roost, they ask about their friends, who's here, who's coming, who's likely to come. Everybody likes everybody—look."

People were dancing the Samba with less amusement, more fire. Its rhythm was beating into their blood; some of them had changed partners; some were talking to friends at the tables while their feet kept up the movement that nothing could stop, no one, only Manuelo.

Pollinger was making his way round the floor, his smile a reflection of the Cuban maestro's, as warm, as carefree, as studied. But it was not false. Business was fine tonight.

At the Bar Copacabaña, Miss Gorringe said:

"So Lady Fireweed is on her way. And asked about you."

"It was nice of her."

"Nice of little Sophie, too. If they arrive here together, Pollinger's slogan of Everybody likes Everybody is liable to ring a fraction hollow. Not that it'll matter, except that small talk will be served with ice."

"It might be interesting. Sophie still wants to

know why I went to Monte with Melody, who wants to know why I went to Sophie's flat last night. One of them's worried, the other is lost."

"Sophie is lost?"

He said: "Yes. I've unsettled her."

"About Brain's death?"

"Yes. She's no longer certain he deserved it. That's breaking her heart. The thing is, when's she going to tell me who killed him?"

"Do you think she knows?"

"I think she believes she knows, but what doesn't quite add up is the fact that she and Struve never had much to do with each other. And we think it was Struve. But does she?"

Vera Gorringe said: "Let's find our table. We're too conspicuous here."

When they were sitting in one of the alcoves opposite the band, she asked him: "If Pollinger is really hiding Struve down here, what does that make Pollinger?"

"A monkey. He'd be assisting a wanted man to evade arrest. But that's his risk."

"Have you asked him about this man Peter Bridges yet?"

"No. I want to ask him in front of Sophie. You never know when someone's silence might make a loud report."

They watched the dance floor until a waiter came. When Bishop had ordered their meal, she asked: "What time does the balloon go up, Hugo?"

"Midnight."

She looked at her watch. "Three hours."

"Yes. It'll be a nice windup to the cabaret . . . at public expense."

The music was sticky. Feet were slower. The bright stimulation of early evening had gone. The band played on. People were no less happy; a few were drunk; a few were sleepy; many had gone. The ordinary licensed bars had closed, an hour and a half ago; it was nearly twelve.

Manuelo was still smiling. His smile ached. Pollinger was helping a man into his car, making sure his chauffeur would be driving.

Melody was dancing with a good-looking Scot. Bishop was sitting at the table in the alcove opposite the band. Sophie and Vera Gorringe were with him. A couple of dozen people were dancing; a group sat on the balcony. The atmosphere of the place had changed from gaiety to a waking reverie. No one was misbehaving; most people were still having fun.

Sophie was moulding a miniature spinning-top out of the wreckage of a bread roll, with the serious concentration of someone not drunk, not sober. She said slowly:

"Poor thing. He beat them all to it."

Nobody at the table had spoken for minutes; she had said it out of the air.

"Who?" said Bishop.

"Geoffrey, of course. He didn't wait to see them all come to pieces. Why did the American shoot—" She broke off and watched the little bread top as it spun on her plate. It fell and was still—"shoot him?"

"Nobody said he did," murmured Bishop. He watched her steadily, idly. "That was just a theory."

"Theories. About everything in the world. Always theories. Like webs, sticky webs. What about facts? Who shot Geoffrey de Whett?"

Miss Gorringe looked at Bishop. He said to Sophie:

"Don't you know?"

Her eyes widened as she looked up at him.

"Why should I? I wasn't there." She focused across the room, watching the Scot and his partner. "Perhaps it was Mrs. de Whett. Quicker than divorce." She smiled about something and looked down.

"That's quite an allegation," said Miss Gorringe.

"Theories and allegations, hypotheses and accusations, about David, and now about de Whett. Doesn't anyone know anything? Or are they scared of saying?"

"Yes," said Bishop.

Her head swung up again.

"They're scared?" she said.

"Of being involved. People don't like to be involved in murder. You don't, or you'd throw one fact into the mass of theories."

"I know a fact?"

"You know who killed David."

Her voice became suddenly taut. "What's it matter who killed him? He's dead."

"Is that all that matters, to you?"

"Yes. Why should anything else?"

He said dryly: "I'd have to start from Cain, to answer that one. Then there are the MacNaughton Rules."

She watched him steadily.

"What are they?"

"They lay it down that if a man murders someone, he has to hang."

"But first he has to be found." He shrugged. She said:

"Very well. We have a police force. It's their job. Why don't they look for the man?"

Bishop said: "They are. That's what they're here for."

She frowned.

"Here? Where?"

He looked across to the doors. He said: "Over there."

The doors were closed. Pollinger was standing inside, talking to Frisnay and another man, explaining something with his hands, trying to rake up the smile from the pit of his panic. Except for the three at this table, nobody in the room had noticed anything. Two men had just come in and were talking to Tom, that was all.

Sophie looked back at Bishop.

"They are police?"

He nodded. She asked: "How d'you know?"

"I just happen to."

She turned her bare shoulders and stared again towards the doors; when she turned back she said:

"Why are they here, Hugo?"

"To look for the man who killed David. I told you."

"But why here? Is he here?" Her eyes were sober.

"That's what they've come to find out."

She said with something like a soft, grave laugh: "I don't believe you. They're not the police." She looked round quickly at the other people. "Nobody's taking any notice."

"If you don't believe it," said Bishop evenly, "try to leave."

She got up. He helped her with her chair. She picked up her bag and walked round the edge of the dance floor.

Pollinger was still talking to Frisnay and his sergeant, but they had moved away from the doors.

Miss Gorringe said quietly: "She's an odd little thing, Hugo."

He nodded. "Scared stiff of something."

"Of the police, apparently."

"It looks like that. I don't know."

Sophie had reached the doors. Frisnay had glanced at her as she had passed the three men. She opened the doors and went out. The doors remained open. When she came back in a few seconds, Pollinger stopped what he was saying to Frisnay and took a step towards her.

"It's quite all right—" he began, and got something of a smile on to his face. She interrupted him.

"There's a man outside the doors. He says I can't leave."

"It's only a routine visit, just routine. It's quite all right. If you'd like to go back to your table just for five minutes—order what you like, on me." His desperate cheerfulness sagged suddenly. "We don't want anyone to get upset." He looked at Frisnay. "Everybody's very happy here—look." His plump hand swept the room, by habit.

Frisnay's voice was like a stone.

"That's quite right," he said to the girl. "Please go back to your table. You'll be allowed to leave as soon as possible."

She looked directly at him and said:

"I'd like to leave now."

Pollinger became anxious.

"Please, Miss Marsham—"

"I want to know why you're here." She said it to Frisnay.

"That's all right," he said in a bored voice. "Now please go back and sit down."

"Are you police?"

"That's right."

She turned away and walked back to the alcove table. Pollinger watched her for a moment and then said:

"You see how easily people get upset when—"

"Yes," said Frisnay. He looked across the heads

of the dancers. "Now I'd like you to show us round, please."

Pollinger looked desolate.

"But it would mean going into people's rooms—people stay here—"

"Stop playing for time, Mr. Pollinger. We'll start with that door on the far side."

The three of them moved off.

Sophie sat down and said to Bishop:

"I don't understand."

"You don't have to. Leave it to them."

"They're being stupid," she said.

She and Vera Gorringe and Bishop watched the three men going through the narrow doorway across the dance floor. In a moment the door closed. People went on dancing, sitting, drinking, talking.

Miss Gorringe murmured: "Freddie has kid gloves on tonight."

"He might have to take them off, if it gets too warm in here." He was watching Melody. She and the big man were swaying together, right by the band, their bodies alone moving in the rhythm, their feet almost still. It didn't seem as if she had seen the two men who had gone out with Pollinger.

He heard Sophie's voice. It was no longer soft and slow. It was cold, sharp, sober.

"Why did you ask Tom about Peter Bridges?"
He looked at her.

"I wondered if Tom had known him. Or knew him."

"You could have asked me."

He said: "Do you know everyone Pollinger meets?"

She looked at him without any expression.

"Talking to you is like dueling." She turned with a sudden slight movement to Vera Gorringe—"Do you find that, too, with Hugo?"

Miss Gorringe said: "It depends on the subject, my dear. And there always has to be a first thrust. This time I don't think Hugo made it."

Sophie glanced back to him.

"Did I?" she asked.

"You said the police were being stupid," he said, "coming in here to look for whoever killed David Brain. I can't agree."

Her voice took on a deliberate lightness.

"You believe they'll find him?"

He said slowly: "Before a raid of this kind is made—and despite the gentle appearance it *is* a raid—a lot of forethought is employed at the Yard. Some policemen have big feet, but none of them has a small brain. If they don't find the person they want at Beggar's Roost, it won't be because there was never the slightest chance of his being here."

She looked at the dance floor.

"Why haven't they started looking in here first? When they raid places, they usually make people line up and give their names and addresses."

He said: "Then they must be certain the man they want isn't dancing tonight, or—"

Miss Gorringe interrupted him.

"Hugo," she said softly.

He glanced at her. She was looking across the room towards the band. She murmured:

"Melody has changed partners."

He turned his head and saw the big Scot moving back to the tables. Melody was still on the dance floor. She was dancing with Struve.

Bishop said: "So she has," and pushed his chair back.

17th

MOVE

♗ HER VOICE was harsh beneath the beat of the band.

"I didn't see anyone."

"But they're here, just the same. Keep dancing. If you stop dancing I'll drill you."

"What are you afraid of, if you don't know anything about Geoffrey?"

"I'm not afraid of anything. Keep moving this way. Towards the balcony."

Manuelo smiled to them as they passed. His smile was strained. He had seen the two men come in. He had seen policemen before and he could recognize them. Pollinger had gone out with them, looking upset. Manuelo was not personally worried; his conscience was clear; his music hadn't missed a beat. But there was a raid going on, quietly and smoothly behind the bright lights and the dreamy faces and the midnight music; and he knew there were places inside Beggar's Roost that the police ought not to see.

Manuelo liked Pollinger. They knew their business, and minded their own. It was going to be Manuelo's business to go on playing his music, in a little while, to make people think there was nothing wrong, if the policemen came back in here and stopped all the joy. It must have been for the hundredth time that Manuelo had taken up his baton tonight in here; and now the place looked like folding.

He smiled at the two nice people who went dancing by. He was already thinking about another job.

He had not heard what they were saying to each other.

"Everett, you won't make it. If they're really here, they'll be here in force. You're hot."

"I'll make it, and you'll make it with me."

"No, darling. I'm sorry, but I choose my men."

"This time it's my choice. I'm taking you or I'm leaving you here—growing cold. Here on the floor. You can believe me. I'm in too deep to worry much either way. But as far as I can I'm going to play it the way I want it to go."

He was not looking at her, but he was smiling

with a cold, calm stare as other people moved into his view. The French doors to the balcony were behind him now. He could hear the voices of the few people who sat out there with their drinks.

He said: "All right. Let's go."

"Don't be a fool." Her hand was like a clamp on his fingers. "If they're here, they're here to get you. You won't manage a dozen yards."

"Just one final word, baby." He looked into her ice-blue eyes. "If I've got to leave you, I'll leave you dead."

His right hand was inside his dinner jacket. She wondered how bad his arm was, if a blow would agonize enough. She knew it wasn't broken; she had felt the strength of his fingers while they were dancing.

"Everett, I'll make an offer. Leave here alone, and go to my place. I'll follow you."

His smile was fixed. "Do I look crazy?"

She looked past his shoulder. He saw her eyes change. When he jerked his head he heard Bishop say:

"This time, Struve, remember your party manners."

Melody shivered as she felt the hard muzzle of the gun press against her body. Struve said:

"Listen, Bishop. The lady and I are leaving. If

you get other ideas, I squeeze." The dull blue metal of the gun pressed harder against the crimson tie-silk of her dress, puckering it. "And how can I miss?"

The band beat on. Manuelo was looking this way. He could see the glint of the dull blue metal, the paleness of the lady's face. All he could do was to go on giving out music until something happened, good or bad. This number would go on for minutes now. It could end on percussion, though the drummer wouldn't know; nor the lady in red.

He smiled with his friendly smile and watched the three people and went on playing his band. He couldn't do anything else.

Faintly he heard the voices at the other end of the dais, but couldn't make out the words.

"There's a ring round the place. You'll run right into it. It's like a big noose."

"The hell with it," said Struve. "I meant what I said, buddy boy, so don't *you* make any mistakes."

She felt needles in her scalp. She knew Everett. She could see his face, and knew its look, had seen it before. His eyes were bright; there was power in his hands; the sense of it was in his eyes, like the effect of a drug.

She heard herself saying:

"Hugo."

The music beat faster. Manuelo was smiling harder. People began laughing, trying to keep up with the band.

"Yes?"

"He means it."

The thing against her body was going off all the time in her mind. The slugs were ripping into her flesh and she could feel them picking her to death.

Bishop said:

"All right."

She released her breath, but the pressure of the gun didn't change.

Struve said: "Fine." He didn't look away from Bishop as he moved in a half-circle. "On your way."

She walked across the edge of the maple floor, on to the carpeting. The pressure was in her back now, an inch from her spine.

Bishop stood at the side of the French doors, waiting for them to go through. His hands hung at his sides. He was watching Struve steadily. Struve said softly as he passed him:

"Raise your hand, or give a shout, or take one step after us, and you'll kill her cold."

For her sake Bishop said evenly: "I understand."

"Bright boy."

She walked on to the balcony. Steps ran down from it to the gardens. Half a dozen people were out here, sitting in the glow of the colored lamps. They'd been drinking for hours, now. They weren't drunk. They were just happy and excited and talking across one another. They didn't notice anything. There was nothing to notice except the warm glowing lights and the air with the scent of flowers in it and the music that came pulsing out from the room like the outermost ripples of a pool.

Struve said:

"Down the steps."

She moved forward.

Bishop stood in the doorway, watching. The steps ran down by a whitewashed wall. Jardin-ières of geraniums hung there, spilling the red blooms against the white like great splashes of blood on the quiet wall.

The music stopped.

Manuelo wiped his brow with an enormous yellow silk handkerchief and gave a wide, white grin to all the nice people on the dance floor. They began drifting back to their tables. He stepped down from the dais and went round the edge of the floor past the windows, making for the narrow door.

Bishop turned his head and said: "Tell them to take care. The lady's in danger."

Manuelo looked slightly upset and hurried through the door.

Bishop looked back to the balcony. Struve's shoulders were still visible. Melody was going down the steps in front of him.

She was not talking. Her mouth was dry. She knew that even if anyone shot Struve from behind, he would squeeze his own trigger. He couldn't live without her, and wouldn't die without her. Nobody could kill him at this moment without killing her too. Even from a bullet his death wouldn't be instantaneous; he would have a fifth of a second left of life, and that would be all he'd want, to take her with him.

When they reached the path below the steps he said:

"Keep close to the wall of the house." His tone was metallic. "Isn't it crazy? No matter where we are we always manage to end up saving each other's lives. . . . "

He looked up as they started along the path, and saw the silhouette of Bishop against the glow of the colored lights. He was standing perfectly still against the rail of the balcony, looking down.

Frisnay's voice sounded from behind him.

"Hugo, what's the position?"

Bishop didn't turn. He didn't want to lose sight of them. Over his shoulder he said:

"Struve's got a gun in her back. I think he'd kill her if anyone tried to stop him getting clear. I don't think he'd mind killing her, but he'd rather take her with him alive. But he wouldn't like to leave her behind, alive. He'd think about it too much, in the condemned cell. Other men with her."

"She's got him in that state?"

"I think so. I'm sure enough of it not to take any chances myself. But, of course, this is your pigeon."

Frisnay stood beside him looking down into the gloom of the gardens. He said:

"Some pigeon."

"Yes. I wish you luck."

"What are you going to do?"

"I'd like to help. Under your orders."

"So that I can take the blame if she gets hurt," Frisnay grunted. "I think I'll go through to the drive at the front and line things up."

"All right." He saw the two shadows near the corner of the building. "I'll follow them. May see you again."

He turned towards the flight of steps. Music was sounding from the ballroom again. Two or three of the people sitting on the balcony laughed suddenly. It was the end of someone's story.

Frisnay went through the French doors. Pollinger was standing just inside, with the police sergeant. Frisnay said:

"Just let everything go on as usual, please. But no one will be allowed to leave yet."

Pollinger found some of his smile.

"That's fine," he said. "That's fine. Count on me." He went over to the dais to tell Manuelo. Manuelo had come to find them before they'd got as far as the private rooms with the green-shaded lights. There was a chance yet. He hadn't known the police were anxious to find Struve. They'd nothing on him there. And if they were too busy with Struve to come back to the private rooms, maybe everything could be tidied up while there was time.

As he spoke to Manuelo, Pollinger had a vision in his mind of Beggar's Roost. The whole rambling place was standing in the path of an earthquake. It could go on standing, or it could vanish, overnight, for him.

When he turned round after talking to the band leader, he couldn't see anything of the police. They had gone out to the drive. If he could tidy the place up before they came back, he could show them all round, tell them how much money he'd spent on the place, how nice it was. And he would offer them a drink. Fine bland Scotch, the best. Make them happy. Everyone was happy here. They should be happy too.

He hurried back to the narrow green door.

In the gardens very little of the light from the windows reached the paths and lawns and trees, and there was no moon. The stars alone kept back total darkness.

Bishop was standing at the edge of the drive, between the ornamental fishpond and the wing of the building. He was watching Struve. Struve was walking slowly over the gravel drive to a Delage coupé. It was Melody's car. She was still ahead of him. She walked easily, her bare shoulders forward slightly, her head down, as if she were thinking deeply and unconscious of anyone else.

Behind the coupé was Bishop's limousine. In front of it was Sophie's Sunbeam-Talbot. Nearer the gates was a black 2-liter M.G. Alongside it was a Wolseley. Another Wolseley was tucked in between two roadsters.

Struve's shoes rasped over the gravel. Melody's gold evening sandals glinted as they moved. From near the two Wolseleys and the black M.G., men watched. They were in plain clothes and there were nine of them. They stood with their hands behind them, not moving, just watching.

No one spoke. The night was quiet. Very faintly there came the sound of Manuelo's music from the far wing of the building; that was all, except for the gritting of stones under Struve's feet. Melody was standing by her car. He stopped. The gun was just touching her spine. Her head was half-turned to look at Frisnay, who was walking across from the porch of the roadhouse. In the faint light her face was pale, her eyes glowed.

Frisnay's voice was loud on the quiet air.

"You'll get so far, no farther. Better if you save yourself a lot of trouble, Struve."

Struve was turning his head slowly, looking in a half-circle across the drive and the terrace and the shapes of the parked cars.

Bishop had made no move from the flagstones near the pond. Frisnay's sergeant was next to him. Under the clear, high stars, the twelve men looked at Struve and the woman, and nobody moved. Frisnay had stopped within a half-dozen yards of the Delage. The scene was strange. They might all have been on location, here in front of the rambling house, standing idly waiting for the cameras to turn, the lights to come on, the director to call for action.

Bishop felt sorry for Frisnay. The situation was

humiliating for him. He had ten men with him.
They had come here to fetch Struve. Now Struve
was in command, and they were having to stand
here and watch him go. If they tried to stop him
they risked a civilian's life. They couldn't do that.
And Struve knew it.

More than ever he realized the power that was
in his hand, and the feeling of its power was in
his voice. He looked at Frisnay as he spoke.

"Listen."

Her spine crept. She was feeling sick. It wasn't
so much the death as the waiting. Her nerves had
been drawing out since Struve had been dancing with her. Now they were like steel strings
trembling at snapping point. Almost she wished
it would go off, get it done with.

"We're getting out now."

His voice sickened her, the elation in its tone,
the triumph. Nothing could be bigger than he
was, at this moment. If one of the twelve men
sprang, if one of them tackled him, if one of
them even struck him from behind and split his
skull, he'd live another fifth-second and his finger would jerk. She was living on the hairspring
of her nerves, and of the gun.

"Now get this. There's not a thing you can do,
any one of you, because my life's at stake, and
yours isn't. Only the woman's, and mine. Mine

267

doesn't matter a red cent to you. Hers does. And mine matters to me. It's very simple. I'm not asking you what you aim to do about it. I'm telling you."

He looked behind Frisnay, then back at him.

"Get your men over by that wall."

Frisnay said:

"It's only a question of time."

"All right, it's a question of time. I like it that way. Tell your men."

Frisnay looked at Melody. He called to her:

"You realize, Miss Carr, that we'll do all we can for you. I'd like you to co-operate by doing whatever this man says."

Her voice was mechanical, dry-pitched.

"Very well."

Frisnay looked round at the waiting men.

"Come over by the wall," he said.

The tableau broke up. Their shadows left the shadows of the parked cars. Their shoes scratched over the loose gravel. Gradually the sound died away, and in a moment there was silence.

Struve said: "And you, Bishop. With them."

The single footsteps sounded along the flagstones. He stopped, standing next to Frisnay by the wall. Frisnay murmured: "Don't do anything free-lance, chum."

"All right."

Struve's voice came.

"Nobody move."

He nudged with the gun. "Get in."

She opened the near-side. He said: "Slide through. You're driving, baby." When she was behind the wheel he climbed in beside her.

A splash of light washed over the terrace and the wall where the twelve men stood; an engine sounded, loudening. A car was slowing, turning in to the driveway. Struve said to her softly: "Hold it."

She sat with her hands on the wheel.

The car doused its headlights, moving at a crawl to the terrace. The man and woman in it were looking at Frisnay's men, standing in a line. Struve waited until the car had stopped and the engine cut out.

The man behind the wheel switched off the sidelights and got out. He said something to the woman with him. She laughed. They were in evening dress. When they were both out of the car, Struve called:

"You two."

They turned and looked at the coupé.

"Get over by that wall, with the others. Fast."

They stood without moving. They didn't know whether this was funny or offensive. They turned again when they heard Frisnay's voice.

"I'm a police officer. Please stand over here. You're in no danger, but this situation is serious."

Again he hesitated. The woman made a little sound of alarm. The man said something to her and then they moved over the gravel towards the wall and the twelve men. Either the girl was of a nervous type, or the strange, quiet presence of the men against the wall unnerved her, for she suddenly began babbling to the man in a thin-toned voice of excitement.

It all blocked in her throat as Struve's shout came.

"*Shuddup!*"

She seemed to be spun round by his voice. The man gripped her wrist and said something quietly. They stood side by side, against the wall, looking towards the coupé.

Struve said in his throat:

"Start up."

She moved automatically. The starter whined and then meshed, spinning the engine. It fired soon. She brought her foot up and let it idle. Struve said:

"Warm up."

She pushed the choke in and gunned the engine on thin mixture, picking up again and again on the throttle as it tried to starve. All the time, Struve was looking past her to the terrace. Against the wall, none of the fourteen people had moved. He hadn't taken his eyes from them since the girl had wheeled round at his shout. He looked at them past Melody's profile as she warmed the engine. He saw in short focus the silhouette of her nose and mouth. He said:

"Look at me."

As she turned her head he kissed her mouth. Her hand braced and her fingers dug into his shoulder and she closed her eyes. It might have been passion, or hate, or the tension of not being able to free herself because of the gun. He did not know. His eyes were wide open and he still stared at the people against the wall, past the dark silhouette of her ear, a lock of her hair.

In a moment she jerked her head away and looked through the windshield, expressionless, light-eyed, pale. Her breath began steadying.

"You and me," he said. "We're going to have fun."

She didn't answer. Her fear was dying. When he had kissed her suddenly like that she had felt the gun pressing into her body, into her side, above the hip bone. She had believed he was going to shoot, kissing her. Men did it sometimes. He'd told her about them, about the friends and enemies he'd known in the States.

Sometimes when a racketeer came to know it was the end, he'd die with a woman, killing her while she held him, then turning the gun on himself.

Struve had smiled, telling her about that. He'd said:

"They've got a point, it's a wonderful death. If I can fix it, that's how I'll crash the gates."

Her breathing was almost normal. She touched the throttle pedal automatically, feeling its hard pressure through the sole of her evening sandal.

He said:

"Let it idle."

The noise died; the regular throb came in, a repeated murmur from the exhaust. Struve called out:

"The first man that comes after us is going to be the man who kills this woman."

The throb of the engine reached the wall, ebbed back in rhythmic echoes.

"Now turn around. Face the wall."

Strangeness came again to the scene. Turning in the faint light, the pale blur of the line of faces was lost against the dark background of the wall. It was as if the fourteen people had shed their identities, becoming anonymous dummies.

Struve said to her: "Lights." She snapped them

on. The drive leapt into stark black-and-white relief through the windshield. He said: "All right, baby. It's all yours."

For an instant she turned her head to look at his face, wanting to know how much chance of life she had. His eyes were febrile. Her lipstick was across his mouth. He was smiling.

The brunt of the gun was painful in her side.

"And don't trouble yourself to drive so fast we'll crack up. You'd be dead before we hit." He looked away from her, to the line of dark figures by the wall. "Let's go."

She jerked the gear lever and clutched-in, sending a rattle of stones flying up from the driveway as the thirty-horse-power engine kicked the wheels into a power spin. Then the treads took a grip and the car went away, the engine pitching up in bottom and then dying, pitching again in second.

Before the sound died on the night air and the glow of light was gone, Frisnay was calling to his men.

"Tucker—the Hayford road. Keep on doubling until further orders. Brown—as far as Sevenoaks, taking in the Wynford bypass—keep in touch till we rendezvous."

Four men were running for the Wolseley near the gates. Three were after them, making for the black M.G. The two remaining patrols and his sergeant were moving with Frisnay for the other Wolseley. Doors were snapping open, starters banging in. Frisnay called a final order before he got into his car.

"Unless you get the all-clear, keep them in sight if you pick them up, and don't do anything more. If they separate, get Struve."

He slammed his door as the driver put the Wolseley into a tight lock. Through the window Bishop called:

"See you at the kill."

"Which one?" But Frisnay's voice was drowned as the car slewed straight and surged for the gates in the wake of the other two.

When the grey Rolls-Royce had gone, swinging left out of the drive and heading for London, silence came back to Beggar's Roost, and nothing was left but the starlight and the bitter-sweet tang of exhaust gas on the air.

18th

MOVE

ALONG THE ditches, tall grass bowed in the car's slipstream, straightened as its gust died and its sound faded. Ahead of it was the white flush of its headlamps. The car was a dark shape for ever straining to enter that pool of light, in vain.

The tires sent up a faint howl as it took a left-hand curve just below sliding-point. The chassis heeled over on the transverse springs. On the dashboard the needle flickered at seventy-plus, climbed trembling to eighty along the straight, fell to below fifty as it slewed into a slow bend with the treads yelling across the macadam and the wheels losing traction to a long controlled drift that took it over to the off side and churned earth from the shoulder before it straightened and sped on.

"Take it easy," Struve said.

"You said go fast."

He looked at her. "And now I'm saying take it easy. Just do that."

She kept her foot on the throttle. The needle began reaching for the eighties again. She said with a trace of excitement in her tone: "You're scared."

He jabbed the gun into her side. It bit into the soft flesh above her hip, making her snatch her breath.

"That makes two of us, baby. Down to sixty."

She lifted her right foot, but still felt the relief of what had happened. He was scared. There was a chink. It was only because he'd come near killing himself that time in the States, but that didn't make any difference. His fright was real. At high speed, he went yellow.

"Everett," she said. Her voice was light above the sound of the big engine.

"Well?"

"We're level." Her right foot was going down on the pedal in fractions of pressure. "You can't do anything. If you shoot, we smash."

The speed touched seventy. The road ran curving between woodland. A car passed them the other way, pulling well over, worried. He said:

"Don't get ideas. Bring it down."

The slipstream went past the side windows in a great singing hiss. The wheel trembled in her hands.

"No, Everett." She turned her head for an instant and snatched a mental image of his face. His lips were dry; her lipstick on them looked brown; his eyes had lost their glow, were ready to flinch.

The gun bit into her body again.

She said: "Shoot, then."

The springs began bucking as she forced the steering over, snaking into a fifty-mile-an-hour bend at sixty-plus. The treads began a hundred-yard scream.

She believed he could kill her in cold blood, and then finish himself with a second bullet, playing the breaks the way he wanted them. But she didn't believe he could just offer both their lives to chance violence that would mangle them slowly, perhaps even let them live on with their bodies distorted and half alive, perhaps for years. That scared him, but not her. Instinct told her that when she died, she would die decently and without doubt, in a crack of thunder. Like David.

"Bring it down," Struve called above the scream of the tires. The slide was taking them wide, the wheels sketching dark streaks across the starlit road. Then the rear swung suddenly and she was fighting at last for their lives, dragging the wheel into the slide and correcting—over-correcting, fighting a counter-skid that slung them back to the near side and sent up a spume of turf from the bank before the springs pitched straight and the dampers held, killing their oscillation.

"Slow, you goddamn bitch!"

She sent the car down the road, her foot aching on the throttle pedal, pressing it flat to the floorboards.

"No, Everett . . . you said go fast!" She was laughing the words out of her throat. The danger was in her blood and her blood was hot with it. This was not like a single finger-movement, a cold, mean bullet. This she could take.

His voice had a brassy pitch; fear was in it.

"I shoot on five! *One. . . .* "

She said fiercely: "All right!"

"Two. . . . "

She bit her lip as the gun dug deep into her side but she held her right foot rigid.

"Three. . . . " Panic in his voice, but now she knew he'd do it, out of panic, out of fear alone, instinctively like a dying wasp that stings blindly.

"Four...." He jerked the word out of a dry mouth and she saw the white blur of his face reflected in the windshield, watching her while the wind went by like a hiss of rage and the engine sang like a friend. The needle touched eighty ... eighty-one ... eighty-two ... but neither saw it, because he was still staring at her face and wondering with a queer, detached part of his mind how it would look when he squeezed the trigger and she felt the slug tearing in, and because she was staring at the web of light that was rising through the trees. She was jabbing the brakes already and Struve's head jerked to look through the window.

"For Christ —" but it was lost in the howl of the tires as she stood on the pedal and tried to pull over. They were going into the bend too fast even with a clear road, and the other car was near the crown. Its lights dipped but the glare was still bad. It began pulling over. She couldn't hope to get the Delage through on the near side so she let the wheel spin straight and went for the gap on the outside of the curve with her lights full on.

Centrifugal force took over and sent the coupé sliding wide at a diminishing fifty under the brakes. Her foot came up, slammed down on the throttle, kicking the car straight and sending it across the grass. For yards the grass was flat; then there were saplings; behind the saplings were bigger trees and a fence.

Struve called something as they cleared the other car and went bucking over the turf. She wrenched at the wheel but the steering just began flapping about in a front-skid with control quite gone. As they hit the belt of saplings the noise was like chopping sticks. The car bounced twice, across a ditch and against a tree stump, then ploughed along the fence and rocked over, sliding to a halt on its near-side.

She fell across him and he flung an arm in front of her face as she lurched and found her feet. He grabbed her hand. The gun dug into her back.

"Run," he said. The word was choked out.

"I can't, I—"

"Run, you bitch!"

As they began going through into the deeper trees they heard the sound of the other car reversing down the road. Their feet cracked among twigs and he caught her twice as she reeled. Orange light glowed from behind them now. The coupé had caught fire.

"Run, goddamn you!"

Her breath rasped out of her. His grip on her

arm had paralyzed the nerve. The orange glow
got brighter but shadows stood across it now, the
shadows of trees. Faintly a voice shouted. They
ran on, blindly now, flinging their hands up to
protect their faces. They ran until she fell head-
long under him.

The shape of the car was indefinable. White
firefoam covered it, mantling it like snow. Behind it was one of the Wolseleys. Two or three
motorists had pulled up. A farmer leaned on a
bicycle, pajamas under his army coat.

Frisnay was standing with his hands in his
pockets when the grey limousine came up and
whispered to a stop on the grass verge.

Frisnay called out: "You got a torch in there,
Hugo?"

Bishop had one in his hand as he got out of
the car and slammed the door. He looked at the
foam-covered coupé as he came up. He asked:

"They dead?"

"No," said Frisnay. He looked at the mass of
trees. "They're in there." A thin man with spectacles was standing beside him. "This gentleman
says they ran that way."

"Yes?"

"I've phoned a request for a cordon, but we

might as well make a start." He turned away to talk to one of his men.

The spectacled man said to Bishop: "They were driving wildly, very wildly. I didn't know what was happening—they just came straight for me." He made a gesture with his hands, very excited about what had happened. Bishop nodded and said:

"Congratulations."

"What?"

"I mean you were lucky. Excuse me." He left the man and picked his way through the belt of saplings, swinging a leg over the fence and looking into the trees. As he dropped on the other side of the fence and began moving forward he heard Frisnay's voice:

"Bishop!"

He turned.

"Yes?"

"He might still have the gun. Your own risk."

"All right, Freddie."

He began moving again, the torch in his right hand, thumb on the button. He had driven some twenty miles behind headlights and his eyes were still accommodating. He went on slowly until it was possible to make out the darker patches that were trees, the lighter places that were clearings; then he went at a better pace for a score of yards, and stopped, steadying his breath, standing motionless, listening.

Small sounds reached him, many small sounds. It was a warm summer night and the wood was alive with them. In the calm of the air it was possible to hear the movement of insects yards distant: the The rasp of a grasshopper, the drone of a gnat, the whisper of things that moved in the undergrowth.

He stood there for minutes. Almost he decided to go back and wait for the cordon to be drawn up, so that he could make one extra; because the chances of his finding Struve and Melody in this wood alone were thousands to one against. He could keep moving for a week of nights among these trees, and pass within feet of Struve without seeing him or hearing him.

The only way to find them was by beating in with twenty or thirty men, unless he had the luck of the devil and stumbled right upon Struve's prone body. Even then, the man would simply shoot him down and run.

There was no point in going on, but he moved again. It was better than standing about waiting for Frisnay's men, perhaps till morning light.

He covered a dozen yards, and stopped. The thudding died away. A rabbit had bolted from almost under him. He moved on, more slowly, his head half-turned so that the slight stirring of air from his own motion should not sound against his ears.

He kept on, with short intervals of standing still, for what he judged to be about an hour. Twice he had disturbed rabbits, once a stoat— by the series of leaping sounds that had followed the first brush of the leaves. For some time now an owl had been calling from above the trees and once he had caught a glimpse of it, a ghostly blur that stopped and then lifted, utterly silent. Not long afterwards a creature had screamed, the thin note of its terror paring the silence like a blade.

He was leaning against a tree bole now, listening, his head turning slowly, his eyes trying to probe the gloom, his ears to pick up the slightest sound that might not be natural here. Minutes passed before he heard one. It was the catch of a man's breath, over to his right, an unmistakable human sound among the hundreds that he had now grown used to in these trees.

The barrel of the torch was moist under the heat of his hand. His thumb eased forward, touching the button, and he held the torch at arm's length beside him. When he pressed the switch it could bring a bullet singing from the dark. He waited, taking quick, shallow breaths.

For minutes there was no sound, then leaves stirred as a leg brushed them.

The sound came from his right again. He believed the man had caught his breath, minutes ago, because he had been pulled up sharply by a bough, or had nearly tripped on a root. Now he was on the move.

Bishop was cursing himself for a fool. It could be Struve, over there, or Frisnay, or one of Frisnay's men. If he called out, and it was Struve, there'd either be a bullet or the sound of running feet. If it was a friend, and Struve was close enough to hear the call, he would move off, warned in time.

There had been little point in coming in here alone. Now that he was here, there was less point in cursing himself. He waited, listening. A minute passed before a sound came—only a minute, but this time it came from behind him. It was much closer than the others.

His nape crept to instinctive fear of the unbelievable, for the man could never have moved in a full circle without a sound in so short a time. Then reason came. There were two of them. Both could be friends; either could be Struve. There was no choice. It was a gamble. He picked the nearer sound, the one that had come from behind him.

In thirty or forty seconds he had managed to turn right round in dead silence. He could see nothing but the total black of the tree trunks and the faint mesmerizing gloom of the spaces between, but his ears were picking up a sound again.

It was a steady sound that was maintained, fading and rising at intervals of seconds. It was human breathing. The man could be no more than a few feet away.

He placed his body so that the tree trunk would offer slight protection if a shot came, and held the torch at arm's length again. Then he pressed the switch.

As the beam of light stabbed out in front of him there was the choke of breath and a dull red flash. A bullet ripped into his sleeve. He saw Melody standing in the flood of light, the gun working in her hand, firing again as he dropped and flung the torch at her body.

Its beam spun and went crazy as he dived for her legs in the darkness and the gun banged again, blindly in her hand. The flash of it burned his eyes and the sound crashed in his head, then he touched her legs and brought her down. The gun was silent.

19th

MOVE

♟ HER BODY writhed under him and his cheek opened to her nails before he caught her wrist and forced it to the ground. As he locked her legs with his own she began cursing him, choking out animal sounds that were hardly intelligible; but there was a name among them. Everett.

"Listen," he grunted, "I'm not Struve. Hugo. I'm Hugo."

She didn't hear or didn't understand. When the torchlight had frozen her with its white glare he had seen wide terror in her eyes. She had shot instinctively. She would have shot at anyone, anything.

He forced his hand across her mouth.

"I'm Hugo," he jerked out again.

Her body went limp.

He did not relax. He didn't know, even now, how much there was between her and Struve. Either of them might be prepared to kill him. The gun had dropped from her hand but she might be playing for time until she could find it on the ground.

Her breath sounded raw and painful.

"I thought it was Everett. Wanted to kill him."

He believed her. The shock of the torchlight in her face and his lunge for her had shaken her too much to let her gasp out anything but truth. He took his hand away from her face and rolled sideways, freeing her legs.

She kept saying: "I thought it was Everett . . . trying to kill him."

"He's gone," he said firmly. "Relax. Get your breath back."

He felt her quivering and heard a kind of muted sobbing from her throat. Her hands were cold when he touched them. He began rubbing them. "Don't worry. Everything's fine."

There were voices now, distant in the trees but coming closer. He recognized Frisnay's. Against the undergrowth pale patches of light were blossoming from the dark. The men were using torches.

"Everything's all right now," he said. The

sounds in her throat had stopped. He felt for her hair and smoothed it back from her brow. "Don't worry."

"I wanted to kill him," she murmured, and he knew now that the sobbing had been of rage. She made no attempt to get up. "He took me, Hugo, with the gun at my head."

"Yes?"

"For the first time. That's why he was so crazy. I thought he meant to shoot me, afterwards, but he just threw it away and left me. He'd gone by the time I found it. I was trying to follow him, to kill him. Then it was you."

The flicker of the torches was brightening, and feet were sounding in the leaves. He straightened up and shouted: "Freddie!"

"Hello!"

The light became concentrated.

When Bishop had heard the two human sounds, one had been made by Melody. The other must have been Struve, because if it had been one of Frisnay's men he would have closed in as soon as the gun had fired.

Silhouettes became defined behind the lights. Bishop called: "Struve was here a few minutes ago. He's lost his gun."

Frisnay shouted: "Keep going in a line—and go hard!"

The torches began jerking. The blue of men's faces went past into the clearing: their feet thudded over the fibrous earth with a hollow drumming sound. Frisnay stood over Bishop and the girl, his lamp deflected.

"She's all right, Freddie."

Frisnay grunted. "What about you?" He turned the torch to the crimson gleam on Bishop's sleeve.

"Not serious." He stood up, helping Melody. Her bare shoulder was grazed. The tie silk dress was torn and grimed with earth. Color was back in her face. He said: "I'll take you home."

"All right."

Frisnay turned to shout as three more men came through the trees from the direction of the road.

"Spread out—keep going hard—Struve is unarmed!"

They answered and ran on. He looked at the girl.

"I'd like to question you, Miss Carr, as soon as you've had some rest. I'll call round."

She combed her dark hair back with spread fingers.

"Anytime. He killed Geoffrey de Whett. He told me."

"Right. You can give me a statement. And I'm

putting a man outside your flat, just in case we don't find Struve tonight."

With a return of her confidence she said:

"Make it a tall one, with dark eyes."

Frisnay said: "Don't worry, you won't see him. Good night, Miss Carr." He bent and picked up Struve's gun.

As he turned away Bishop said: "See you in the morning, Freddie."

"I'll ring you."

She was limping as Bishop walked beside her. His torch was flickering; the fall had damaged it.

"I've lost a shoe," she said. She stopped and slipped the other one off, throwing it into the bushes. "There's no point in keeping this one."

"I'll carry you to the road, if you like."

"Let's not get romantic. How bad is your arm?"

"It's only skinned."

The torch flickered right out and he had to bang it against his palm before they could go on. Without it, after watching its light, they couldn't see a yard.

"I nearly killed you," she said.

"Yes."

"Sorry."

"You always said you wanted to hurt me."

"I didn't know you very well then."

"Don't tell me you're growing soft."

"I've just grown to like you."

He helped her through brambles, remembering how he had done this before, when they had climbed the earth slope from the hollow in the trees, Brain's grave.

He said: "Why did Struve shoot de Whett?"

She walked a little behind him; he turned.

"It doesn't make any difference to you, does it, Hugo? Whether I like you or love you or hate you, it's just the same, nothing registers."

He stopped. The torch beam hit the ground and cast only a faint glow on her face.

"You're so changeable. When a man comes near you he doesn't know if he's going to be seduced or shot at. That makes him worry."

"You don't worry about a single damned thing in the world." Her eyes were shining and her face was tilted up to his.

"Great grief," he said, "you recover like a steel spring, don't you?"

"You've a recuperative personality. With you near, I like living. If you'd been here, and not Everett, you wouldn't have needed a gun."

He kissed her mouth and said in a moment: "Behave."

She walked on with him.

"Damn you," she said lightly.

"You're welcome."

They came to the fence and he lifted her over. Her body was warm and lithe in his arms. It wasn't credible that she had come twice near death tonight, once in the overturned coupé, again with Struve and his gun. It didn't mean anything to her. She was alive all the time, however close death came. Only when it came finally would the spirit go out.

He dropped over the fence and went with her through the saplings. A constable in uniform was posted near the burned-out coupé. He asked:

"Have they got him, sir?"

"Not yet."

The man looked at Melody. In the light of the two road-lanterns she looked strange with her torn dress and stockinged feet and wild, dark hair. She got into the Rolls-Royce and Bishop shut the door.

The constable helped him turn the limousine across the grass. When it was gliding in top gear along the winding road he said again:

"Why did Struve shoot de Whett?"

"Because of me." She was smiling. "You can tell me I savor the thought. I do. Geoffrey wouldn't mind."

"It's so easy to say the dead don't mind. How can they?"

She said nothing. He said: "Why did Struve kill him—out of jealousy?"

"Yes, or one of its subtle variants. For a long time Geoffrey kept clear of me because of David. David would have killed any man who got within yards of me—that's why Everett kept his distance, too."

Bishop said: "Or partly."

She glanced at him.

"All right, there was the other thing."

"De Whett kept clear of you because of Brain, yes. And then?"

"When David died, he began thinking about me again. Struve told me, on the plane home. Geoffrey is—was my husband, and said he was going to come back to England and ask me to live with him again. Everett blew up and there was trouble at Geoffrey's villa."

The great car swung left and curved through a traffic circle, its headlamp beams flooding across the signboard LONDON.

"Trouble. You mean de Whett was shot."

"Yes. The villa was right on the coast. The body wasn't found until evening—"

"How do you know?"

"The police phoned me, asking a lot of questions, if I knew where Everett was, when did I last see Geoffrey."

"Did they wonder why you didn't sound very surprised that your husband had been murdered?"

"The police never wonder. They just ask. That's what I like about them."

For a while there was silence until he said:

"Why did Struve kill David Brain? For the same reason?"

He saw the reflection of her face turning to him in the windshield.

"That's all wrong, Hugo. He was in the States when David crashed."

"No, he wasn't. He was in London."

"I don't believe it."

"He flew in the day Brain crashed."

Her voice was excited.

"He told me he arrived two days before the inquest. He came straight to my flat. He was lying?"

"Yes."

"Why?"

"Because he killed Brain. That was the last thing he wanted you to know."

She stared back at the road, watching the twin rear lights of a car that was losing ground to their pace.

"Hugo, he might have landed over here before David died, but he didn't kill him. You know

that, better than anyone. The car just crashed.
You saw it."

"I didn't see everything. I was blinded by his
lights."

"But Everett couldn't have been there. The
next car you saw was mine."

"Yes. He wasn't there, but he killed Brain." He
dipped his headlights, taking their dazzle off the
mirror of the saloon in front. "Struve had a motor
smash just after the war, in America. You know
about that?"

She nodded. "Yes. I flew across to see him when
he was in the hospital."

"What caused him to crash?"

She said: "The hood flew up. It wasn't locked
properly when he'd started off."

"And when he got up speed the wind caught
it?"

"Yes. It was like a sudden black-out. He was
doing eighty and was driving blind."

"Yes, of course." He went past the smaller
saloon and then slowed, pulling up a hundred
yards ahead of it. He was standing in the road
when the lights came sweeping down against
him. It was the Sunbeam-Talbot. The tires murmured faintly under the brakes. When it had
stopped, he went over to it.

"Hello, Gorry."

She looked out of the near-side window. Sophie was getting out, slamming the door. She asked:

"What happened, Hugo?"

"Struve got away. I don't imagine for long."

Miss Gorringe said: "Is Melody all right?"

"Yes."

Sophie said: "We passed the burned-out car. Wasn't anybody hurt?"

"No." He leaned his arm along the window ledge and said quietly to Vera Gorringe: "Struve crashed in America because the hood of the car flew up."

"Is that so?"

"Melody's just told me. I don't think she knows he unlocked the hood of Brain's Ventura the night he died. She thought he arrived in London a couple of days before the inquest. So far, she's clear."

"For someone who comes so close to death so many times, she's also fortunate. Are you taking her home now?"

He nodded, straightening up.

"Yes. I'll be in soon after you. We'll have breakfast and then turn in."

"Anything for a change."

As he stood back from the car Sophie said:

"Are they still after Struve?"

"Yes."

"Will they get him?"

"I should think so."

She stared at him for a moment, silent, then: "They believe he murdered David?"

"We're pretty certain now."

"But that's stupid."

"All right. He can tell them that at the trial. By that time, you won't be in a position to protect him any longer."

Her surprise looked genuine.

"Why should I want to protect him?"

"Only you know that, Sophie."

"It isn't true. I just know that it wasn't Struve."

He said evenly: "Then your evidence will be invaluable to the defense. Will you offer it, officially?"

She shook her head.

"No."

"Then I'll forget what you've told me, and leave it to your conscience. The night before they hang him, I hope you sleep."

She opened the door of her car.

"Good night, Hugo."

He raised a hand as they drove away. Miss Gorringe had heard what the girl had said: he could leave it to her to press the subject. He went back to his own car and got in.

Melody was smoking a cigarette. He started the engine.

"I'm tired," she said. She sat curled up on the seat.

"It's been a busy night."

"I'm tired of death."

He moved into top gear, leaving the country road and coming to suburbs.

"There'll be another one yet."

She asked: "Whose?"

"Nobody knows yet. But the jury will."

"There'll be no trial, darling. There's no evidence." She spoke almost drowsily, inhaling the smoke and watching the lights through the windshield. "There's no motive, and not even suspicion against me. I loved him, didn't I?"

He said: "I'm helping the Yard. You know that. If you'd killed Brain, you'd never tell me."

"It's your word against mine, Hugo. They couldn't convict on that."

After a time he asked: "Is this why you're so sure Struve didn't do it?"

"Yes."

Street lamps came swinging out of the dark perspective of the road, glowing across her eyes. She closed them.

"If they put Struve on trial for his life," he said, "what will you do?"

"Nothing."

"Because it'd be his life or yours?"

"Partly. Also I hoped I was killing him tonight, when I shot at you in the wood. What's the difference between a bullet and a rope, except for the waiting?"

20th

MOVE

FRISNAY TURNED in his swivel chair and looked at the guttering at the top of the building opposite his window. Martins had built a nest there, months ago, and now the young had been born and were gone. It made him conscious of time. He was beginning to think it was just a circle, like the philosophers said.

"He won't stay free very long," he told Bishop.

"They might not get him alive."

Frisnay shrugged.

"That's up to him. Orders are to save his neck . . . for the judge."

"You can give him straight to the Public Prosecutor, once he's caught?"

Frisnay turned his head.

"We hope so."

"What does that mean?"

"We hope to get a confession."

"You don't think there's enough factual evidence yet to convict him?"

Frisnay said: "*Just* enough . . . and sometimes that's worse than none at all. Trials are expensive in time and money. And once you acquit a man by giving him the technical benefit of doubt, you've lost him for good."

Bishop watched the tobacco burning at the top of the meerschaum-bowl. The brown strands were curling, glowing, turning grey.

"How much have you got against him, Freddie, without his possible confession?"

"He crashed in the States because the hood of his car flew up and caused a visual blackout at high speed. It was an accident. But we have his finger prints on the hood latch of Brain's Ventura. We have the evidence of first-class mechanics that the hood must have been open when that moth flew in and was crushed to death. We have the evidence of an authoritative insectologist that the moth was traveling at a minimum of fifty miles an hour, for that degree of damage to have been caused to the structure of the head. So we can offer to the jury that the hood of the Ventura was open when it crashed—*before* it crashed. Even though you—

Hugo—didn't see it, because his lights were blinding you."

He folded his hands, staring at the nails.

"The case is simply that Struve came to London to go after Brain. He trailed him to Melody Carr's flat, and saw the Ventura standing outside. He remembered the cause of his crash in the States that nearly killed him. He took a chance—a chance that couldn't possibly do him any harm, could possibly do a great deal of good. If Brain happened to be going anywhere in a hurry when he came out here to his car, the wind might lift the hood at a moment when good visibility was vital—turning a bend, overtaking, something like that. Brain might be maimed or killed. If not—then Struve had come to London with a plan in his mind anyway; a plan that would connect him more closely to the dead man—because all killers are joined to their dead by their own doing, and I speak factually. If this chance failed—the chance of killing Brain without the slightest suspicion against him—then he'd simply go ahead with his original plan. So he turned the hood lock, and left."

In the silence Bishop watched his friend. Freddie was worried. If this had been murder, it was going to be difficult to bring it home. But it had to be done.

303

Frisnay took a breath and finished.

"Struve was in luck. Circumstances of which he was ignorant combined to his advantage. When Brain came out to his car he was under the influence of drink; if the hood gave any slight rattle or bumping before he reached Knoll Hill, his wits weren't sharp enough to notice. Again, he was driving very fast, and probably his highest speed was reached going down the long straight approach to the hill—the approach that makes that hill such a danger spot, because it invites speed. At that speed the weight of the Ventura's hood was nullified by the rush of air, and it lifted. He was suddenly driving blind."

He leaned forward with his clasped hands flat on the desk. Slowly he said: "If that made Brain crash, then it was murder. And the hood release was the murder weapon. Struve's prints are on it. And even if Brain had not been killed, murder was *intended*. What have we as an overall picture? Struve, on whom the deceased had a dangerous hold, was unnaturally influenced by desire for the woman with whom the deceased was associating very closely. He landed in this country with a double motive for murder. On the same night, the man who is the subject of this double motive is killed. Struve's prints are found on his car—and this is the first sign of him in this country since he left the airport, because for some reason . . . he had gone underground."

He leaned back, shrugging. "Hugo, that case is damning, here in my office between the two of us. But the evidence is wholly circumstantial, and juries don't like that."

There was silence again. After minutes, Bishop said:

"You'd be handing over a charge of murder that might be hard to prove?"

"Yes. But that might be better than waiting about to get more evidence: and what more evidence is likely to turn up? We've already questioned some few hundreds of people, any one of whom might have seen Struve near the Ventura when it was standing outside Melody Carr's flat on the night of the crash . . . but none of whom actually did."

Bishop pressed the ash down in his pipe, so carefully that he might have given up all interest in the discussion. Then he said: "What about de Whett?"

"There's even less evidence against Struve from that quarter. I had great hopes, because that killing seemed less complicated. But ballistics here have checked on the bullet in de Whett's body and the gun I brought back from the wood last night. They don't tie up."

"He threw the murder gun into the sea, along with the body?"

"Or somewhere. Only a fool would fail to. We have your evidence that Struve shot at you in your hotel and that his arm was in a sling; in other words he was a man who was ready to fire at anyone he didn't like, and he had some reason for pretending that his arm was temporarily out of action. We have Melody's evidence that he actually told her, last night, that'd he'd killed de Whett. It's all very suspicious, like the Brain case: but it's all very loose. It would tighten, I've no doubt; but I'm being prodded from above. They want Struve on trial as soon as there's just enough evidence. And as I say, there is . . . just enough. So that's my answer. Yes, we hand him over to the Public Prosecutor the minute he's caught."

He reached for a cigarette from his jacket that hung on the stand behind him. The match rasped in the silent room. Smoke edged up to the open window in grey layers and then swirled out to the sunshine. He sat down again, flicking the match end into the ash tray on the desk.

"Why did you want to know?" he asked quietly.

"Because this morning I had a confession of murder made to me, Freddie. Somebody thinks they killed David Brain."

Frisnay gave him a steady X-ray stare and waited.

"I'm going to see them again," said Bishop slowly, "tonight. I'm going to try to get evidence from them. But I don't think it'll be evidence that could be substantiated by any practical methods; and that's why I believe they'll give it to me. It'll be my word against theirs."

After a while Frisnay grunted, looking away.

"If you think you've got anything worth going into, I know you'll let me have it."

"Of course." His hand was stroking his face, subconsciously, his finger tips following the light scar that was just beginning to heal, from the left eye to the chin. When she had taken him to Monte Carlo, she was seeing him as Brain. When she had struggled under him in the heart of the wood, she had thought he was Struve. It was time she took him at his own face value, and he'd make her do that tonight.

He got up, putting the chair against Frisnay's desk. His right arm had stiffened slightly since this morning.

"Meanwhile, Freddie, you'll let me know if you get Struve."

"Naturally. The moment he comes in."

———

Afternoon sunlight was in the room. It cast the carving of the heavy chair into crisp relief, and made shadow-play of the shapes on the limed-oak desk: the ivory telephone, the Chinese jade figurines, cactus plant, paper weights, tobacco bowl, pipe rack, books, boxes of matches ... the orderly antique junk shop that Miss Gorringe attended to daily with a kind of loving exasperation.

Shadows fell also from the figures on the chessboard. Their arrangement was different now.

Miss Gorringe was behind her smaller desk, watching Bishop as he brooded over the checkered squares. He said:

"The thing looks as if it's gone to pieces. It's anybody's game." He had taken away the chessmen they had used for their last tournament, leaving only the symbols of the Brain case. The red King stood as before, in the center of the board: Brain himself, still the figure round which the others turned. Now he moved the red Queen to oppose the King. Before, she had stood beside him.

"Everett Struve," he murmured, "has changed color." He took away the white Knight and replaced it with a red, checking the King and threatening equally the Queen. The other

Queen, the white one, he held in his hand.

"Little Sophie Marsham—"

"A problem child," said Miss Gorringe.

"Ye-es. Still don't know her strength."

He put the white Queen in opposition to the red King, because of the massacred squadron, and at the edge of the board placed a pawn.

"Geoffrey de Whett, deceased. A dead pawn that never made a move."

Miss Gorringe said: "By tonight the picture is liable to be much clearer. For one thing you're seeing Melody. For another, they might have got Struve."

He stood up, scraping the caked ash from his pipe.

"That's true—but will it help?"

"You've had a confession from Melody. You might manage to get evidence. There could still be a confession from Struve, and a certain amount of evidence is already available."

He shrugged. "Suppose I'm convinced—by what she tells me tonight—that Melody in some way killed Brain? Can I convince the police? If not, can they go ahead and put Struve on trial, knowing that they could also put Melody on trial if only they could produce evidence?"

"Freddie would be in a fix."

"He's in one now."

She reached for one of her files. "So are we, about this man Peter Bridges. I don't think there's much hope of finding him, Hugo. There's been no trace of him in this country for the last two years. The Air Ministry has lost track of him altogether."

"What about the names of the squadron?"

"So far I've about half of them. The rest are coming in. But you know what it's like getting unofficial information from official sources, especially when the incident was a matter for an inquiry."

"If anyone can get it, you can."

"Thanks for the burden of your trust in my genius. Hugo, just how much chance is there of Struve's going to trial?"

"Every chance, if they pull him in alive. But a conviction's another matter."

"That sounds odd, when we believe he's responsible for two deaths."

He said: "You can't hang a man twice."

"You think Brain was murdered twice."

"That's rather different." He sat down again behind the desk. "Murder's illegal, and there are no rules."

He stared for minutes at the pieces on the chessboard, then on a thought, picked up his telephone.

Her dark hair was piled high, clasped by Spanish combs. The graze on her shoulder was hidden by a black lace stole. She watched him over her glass.

"So they haven't found him yet."

He said: "No."

"I think that when they do, they'll find him dead."

He stood by the window, looking down into the street. Trees bordered it, sheltering gardens. Two or three cars were parked in the shadow of their leaves. The Ventura had stood there, the night Brain had been in this room. Now there was the grey Rolls-Royce in its place, Bishop in place of Brain. The link, even now.

"You mean he might take his own life?"

"If he's in a corner. But he'll try to reach me first."

He turned. She was lying along the divan, her head pillowed on one arm. Light from the ceiling was refracted through the drink in her other hand, and focused a splash of color against the stole.

"I think you're wrong, Melody. If he'd meant to take you with him, rather than think about you in the death cell, he'd have done it last night. He had the gun."

Bitterness came to her voice, as it had done when she had talked to him in the hotel in Monte Carlo.

"You're forgetting, darling. Once they've taken me, they lose interest. Sometimes within minutes. Remember, he just walked away...."

He moved from the window and sat on the foot of the divan, cupping his drink in both hands and looking down at it.

"I think he threw the gun away and left you because he didn't trust himself. He didn't want to shoot you out of hand. He wanted to save you ... from himself, for himself. He'll come here for you."

"You're trying to scare me." She watched him with cold eyes.

"You're not scared of Struve."

"I was last night."

"But now you know he wants you alive."

She said: "If he comes here, he'll be taken. There's a man below, waiting just for him."

"You hope he'll come, and be caught?"

"Darling, I'm not interested what happens to him. As long as I don't see him again. If he came here for me, and managed to dodge the plain-clothes man down there, I'd turn him in myself."

"He's wanted for murder."

"So?"

"You say he didn't murder Brain."

She finished her drink before she answered him.

"You know he didn't, Hugo. You know it was me. You knew it even before I told you, because for days you've been trying to find out how. But surely it's not very difficult."

She sat upright, giving him her empty glass. He put it down for her. She said with a harsh amusement in her voice: "That little man in the coroner's court was trying to make out a case against me, remember? I didn't let him—why should I? He didn't know my motive even for culpable negligence, even less for murder. But you do."

He said: "And so does Sophie Marsham."

She nodded quickly. "Yes, she knows it too. She even provided it, by trying to take David from me. Already he'd begun drifting a little, just as the others had, but he was still in my hands until she moved into the picture. She'd known him for years—they met after the war— but now she was serious. And so was he. They'd planned to go abroad, the day after he died. To Paris, to get married. He told me." She laughed suddenly, low in her throat. "It was rather pathetic. He sat where you are now—it's odd the way you follow him even in small instances—and he

said we needn't stop seeing each other. When
he was back in England we could meet again
sometimes, just as we were meeting now."

He didn't move his position. He was used, by
now, to walking in Brain's shoes. This was the
room where Brain had spent his last hour, tak-
en his last drink, kissed the last woman in his
life. When he had left this room, he had left an
answer to his death: one answer. There were
others.

"Hugo, he wanted to make me his mistress.
Someone to play with when he got bored with the
better things. My God . . . I could have been mistress to a dozen men, even the death of them."

Anger was in the light cold blue of her eyes.
That night, fury must have been there. Had Brain
been too drunk to see it?

"What did you do?" he asked quietly.

"Do?" She left the divan with a movement as
lithe as a cat's. The anger had gone to her limbs.
"I loved him more than I'd loved any man in my
life, more than it could ever be in me to love
again. And he was going."

She stood against the windows, facing him.

"He was going the next day. To her. What did
I *do*?"

He leaned his shoulders against the wall, his
head half turned. Steadily he said:

"You say you killed him. But how did you kill him?"

Silence lengthened to a full minute as she gazed at him. He broke it softly.

"You're wondering how much you're risking, in telling me what you're burning to tell me. You want me to know how you took him away from the other woman, because it was a triumph for you. You're still heady with it. But how safe are you, in my hands, once you've told me what I've tried to find out since the night we met?"

Her voice was strong.

"I'll always be safe, from you or anyone. I'm not telling you anything that you've not thought of for yourself. At the inquest, it would have been in everyone's mind, if they'd known I had a motive for killing David."

She moved forward slowly towards him, her hands held out a little from her sides, almost appealing that he should understand.

"He'd been under the strain, Hugo. He wanted to go to Sophie, for life. He said he loved her, but he was really in love with me. He'd been on a knife edge for months, and now she'd made him choose. He'd chosen her. He came here for the last time freely, and he knew what I'd say—that if he went back to her, he'd never see me again. That was the strain. He wanted her desperately, but he couldn't face leaving me and all I meant. That's why he'd been drinking more than usual. When I asked him if nothing would make him change his plans, he said it was too late. He was leaving for Paris the next morning."

A smile moved her mouth, unwillingly. She stood looking down at Bishop, her hands slack by her sides.

"I took it well, Hugo. I went very gay. I said we'd one night more at least. We could spend it at Beggar's Roost. He said fine. We had some more drinks and got very happy together and I phoned Tom Pollinger, to say we were coming but I didn't know when because we were a fraction lit. Then we left here together. He wanted to drive me but I said no."

She looked away from him, going slowly back to the window. "I said let's make a race of it—and champagne for the winner at Beggar's Roost."

The lamps below cast a flush on the window. Her silhouette stood against it, absolutely still. He watched her for a little time, then she heard his voice behind her.

"You believe you killed him like that?"

She swung round and almost laughed.

"Oh, God, no! It was an accident—wasn't that the coroner's verdict? When David left here he was drunk. At any time he was a fast driver. Knoll

Hill is a danger spot and it was right on our route. He'd been challenged to a race and he'd accepted it. But accidents happen, and he died. . . . "

He got up from the divan and put down his glass, toying with an ornament that stood on the wall table. It was an ebony sculpting smaller than his hand.

"You must have felt good, Melody, that night. In among the bad, I mean."

Her voice was low.

"I don't remember how I felt. But I know that when I came down the hill and saw the break in the fence I felt as if magic had happened. For a minute I felt like God."

When he turned away from the ornament and looked at her he saw that her eyes were bright.

"Cain," he murmured.

"God or Cain, he'd smashed. David was mine, for always."

She drew a breath and her body relaxed its tension.

He moved and stood beside her, looking down from the window.

"Do you ever wish you hadn't done that?" he asked quietly.

"There hasn't been time yet. One day I might, but I don't think so. He went out when he was magnificent, and that's how I shall always remember him. Magnificent, and mine."

"It's going to be a one-sided lifetime. Isn't it?"

"No, not very. When I'm with other men, now, it's in the dark, and it's David. It'll always be like that."

Half to himself he murmured: "That's why you've hidden your pride so many times, with me, asking me to take you. You couldn't have done that with any other man."

"No. Only you, darling."

She touched his hand. His skin crept and he moved it away, putting his hands in his pockets and looking at her directly; but it was a moment before he could clear his mind of the image, the memory of the mangled thing that had sat behind the steering wheel in the moonlit wood. He was the link between that cadaver and this vital woman; and she wanted him because of it.

"I think I'll go now," he said.

Her voice was flat.

"Very well."

As he reached the door she said:

"Hugo."

"Yes?"

"What are you going to do?"

"About what?"

"About me."

"Forget you," he said.

21st

MOVE

♟ THE SPEEDOMETER needle was steady
at seventy as the great grey car came
into the straight. Within seconds the headlamp
beams picked up the red triangle, then the special sign that read: *STEEP HILL—Gradient* 1 *in*
9.

Bishop slowed. His car took the first curve
at less than forty. The lights sent the mass of
leaves lime-green, throwing their shadows to
the chalk bank, draping it with a web of lace.
On the third curve of the hill there was no break
in the black-and-white board fence. The only difference was that a line of red reflectors glowed
along the lower half of the posts. The jury had
recommended it.

He turned his eyes and saw the fork in the road, where the way to East Knoll branched off below the curve. The signpost whitened in the rush of light, then darkened as the Rolls-Royce left the hill and sped on southwards to Telbridge.

In twenty minutes the windows of Beggar's Roost were in sight, blossoming from the dark background of the trees like pale oleanders against the hillside. The tires crackled drily over the gravel drive. He doused the lights, nosing into a space between the Sunbeam-Talbot and a low slung roadster.

Sophie was sitting alone in the South Lounge, reading a magazine.

"Hello," he said. "Sorry I'm late."

"Are you?" She studied him gravely for a moment, then smiled. "As long as you came. Last night you seemed so cross with me. Now you're not."

"Last night was a trifle fraught with psychological unexploded bombs. Some of them even went off. What would you like?"

"Pimm's, please. Thirsty."

He turned away. She said: "Don't hurry. I've rung."

"It's all right, I've got to telephone."

He met a waiter coming in, and ordered the drinks, going on to the phone booths in the hall.

Miss Gorringe answered within seconds, once he was through.

"Hugo," he said.

"Where are you?"

"Beggar's Roost. I felt like a breath of fresh air."

"How was Lady Fireweed?"

"Very well. I can't say very much over the phone, but I'm afraid Freddie has a headache coming. It's going to be a very difficult thing to pin down. Any news?"

"Yes, Hugo."

He listened carefully, making a note with his pen. When she had finished he said:

"All right, Gorry." He looked at his watch. It said half-past ten. "I shall be back probably in the early hours."

"Very well. If Freddie telephones, what shall I say?"

"It depends on whether they've got Struve, but in any case I think we'll have something for him by morning. If he can call round, we'll put everything on the table for him, together with a bottle of aspirins."

"I'll suggest that, if he rings."

"All right, Gorry. 'Bye."

He left the telephone booth and went out to the drive. It was quiet. A shadowy herd of cars was gathered opposite the terrace, but no one was out here. He went across to his car, glancing back once to the terrace before he bent down and unscrewed the valve cap of a rear tire, reversing it and loosening the valve core. Air began hissing faintly in the silence. In a moment he straightened up and walked back to the building.

On his way to the lounge he saw Pollinger ahead of him. The man's face came apart for an instant and he glanced over Bishop's shoulder. Then the smile came.

"Well, hello!"

"Don't worry, Pollinger, I'm just here for a peaceful half-hour."

The smile took on a little sincerity.

"I'm glad. That's fine, fine. I hope we both mean the same thing when we say 'peaceful'. Last night you just came for dinner and dancing, and we had everything here but bombs."

They walked together into the lounge.

"I'm sorry. It was necessary. There was a wanted man here, and he was dangerous."

"Lots of people are dangerous."

They stopped near a group of Pollinger's special friends. Everyone at the Roost was Pollinger's special friend. Even Mr. Bishop, the smile said.

"One thing I'd like you to know," Bishop said. "Since you first showed me round here, I've had quite a lot of nice hospitality. If I were any kind of official, that wouldn't make any difference, but I'm not." His voice became a murmur. "Last night the police came to raid the Roost and look for Struve at the same time. It was my idea that Struve might be gone to ground here, and he was wanted for murder. I told the Yard what I thought. But about the backrooms you might or might not have here . . . it wasn't my tip. They knew about them before."

Pollinger looked at him with his balding head tilted and his black, shiny, robin's eyes peeking brightly at Bishop's face.

"I believe you," he said.

"Good."

Bishop moved on, half-turning his head: "Now they admit officially that there's something here to raid, they might come again."

Pollinger beamed.

"They'll be most welcome. I'd like them to see the place. Show them round. Right round. Everywhere."

Bishop smiled faintly and walked away. A lot of people were going to be disappointed. They'd have to start backing horses now. That was legal. For some reason, that was all right, where the wheel wasn't. But then he didn't make the laws.

"Tom's very happy tonight," Sophie said.

He sat down with her. Their drinks were on the table.

"Yes. But then everybody's happy here—look!"

She laughed at his faithful rendering.

"Tom's nice," she said. "He keeps out of people's way." She took up her drink. He said:

"To you."

"Thank you."

She watched the people for a minute, idly. He was looking at her when she turned.

"I was glad when you asked if I'd be down here, Hugo. Last night I was a little drunk, and probably made a nuisance of myself—"

"That's absurd. We all had a nice time."

She looked down.

"There was a great deal going on that I didn't know about, wasn't there?"

"Perhaps. And a great deal that you did know about. But we'll leave it. That was last night. Tonight is different in a lot of ways. Times have changed, in a few hours."

"They've found Everett Struve?"

"Not yet, as far as I know."

"But they will?"

"I think so, yes."

"He'll be charged with murder?"

"Probably."

She said nothing for a time. Then:

"How soon would the trial be, if it got that far?"

"Months."

She gave a slight shrug. "In months, anything can happen, can't it?"

"It can happen in minutes."

Some people stopped near their table and said hello to her. She talked for a moment and introduced Hugo before they moved on.

She said to him: "People are crowding in tonight. They've heard about the raid and hope there'll be another impromptu *divertissement*. Shall we talk somewhere less crowded?"

"In the grounds?"

She nodded. They finished their drinks.

Music filled the ballroom and half the building. It was midnight and Manuelo was full of moonlight. Business was bright. You couldn't play the wheel anymore, but Beggar's Roost was a place where things happened. People came to see.

Two of them were leaving. Miss Marsham and Mr. Bishop. As they went through the hall, a waiter came up.

"Mr. Bishop?"

"Yes."

"Telephone, sir. Booth Three." He led him away.

The air pressed as he drew the door shut.

"Hugo?"

"Yes."

"Freddie. Gorry told me where to find you. Struve is in." He sounded pleased.

"Alive?"

"Of course. We always get 'em alive."

"You sound very gay."

"The man's been a worry. He got within a couple of miles of Melody Carr's place."

Bishop watched Pollinger go past the glass door.

"I'm happy for you, Freddie."

"You don't sound it."

"Listen—where are you lunching tomorrow?"

"At my favorite banqueting-hall. It's just behind my desk. I just sit there, lounging away both minutes of my lunch hour, which—"

"Take longer tomorrow," said Bishop. "Have it with Gorry and me."

"I'd like to. Where?"

"My flat. Partly business."

"I don't like your tone. It's muffled, as if you're tugging the pin out of a grenade with your teeth." He sounded worried about it.

"No, I've nothing much for you, Freddie. Just the odd item that might help you frame the whole picture. Come about twelve-thirty."

When Frisnay rang off, he asked for London. Melody's telephone rang for half a minute before she answered.

"This is Hugo."

"So you haven't forgotten me yet." Her tone was lazy.

"That will take time. I rang you to say that Struve has been picked up."

There was a brief pause.

"Yes?"

"I thought you'd be glad."

Her voice had lost its laziness, was cold.

"I am."

"It must be wonderful for your ego."

"I don't understand."

He said: "They found him within two miles of you. He was trying to reach you."

"Why should that do anything to my ego?"

"Just the thought. They risk even the rope, to get to you."

The pause was longer.

"No, Hugo. After the first few deaths, devotion bores. But thank you for letting me know." She said good-bye and hung up.

When he found Sophie on the terrace he said: "Sorry."

"Is everything all right?"

"It depends. Struve has been caught."

He was watching her face. The soft light from the windows glowed on it, shone in her eyes. She looked up at him for seconds.

"I see. I suppose it was inevitable."

"Yes."

She gave a shiver, looking away.

"It's not pleasant to know that a man's in a trap, suddenly."

"But you think he'll get out."

"I don't know. If he killed Geoffrey de Whett, then he deserves to die. You were trying to explain something about that, last night. I was obstinate."

"Whether he killed de Whett, or Brain, or both, isn't it the same?"

She looked at him once, quickly.

"He didn't kill David."

She moved suddenly. They went down the three steps to the drive. As they reached their cars she pressed his hand.

"I've enjoyed almost all of tonight, Hugo. When we were just talking about ourselves."

She seemed very small against him, very grave, with large, calm eyes looking up into his face.

"I'm sorry other things got in the way," he said gently. "They won't always." She released her hand. He said: "If you get a puncture on the road, I'll be right behind."

She opened the door of her car and got in. He closed it for her and moved round to his own.

"Sophie," he said.

Her face was in the window.

"Yes?"

He was looking at the rear of his limousine.

"The devil made me say that. I've got one myself."

She peered round at the flat rear tire.

"Bad luck. How's the spare?"

He put his hands into his pockets.

"One's flat, too. The other's being fixed in town. If I start mucking about with patches and bowls of water it'll be morning before I'm fit."

"Tom would put you up."

He looked at his watch.

"I've got to be in town quite early."

"Then leave it here for them to fix. I'll run you home."

"That'd be sweet of you. I'll go and ask Tom to phone a garage for me, first thing tomorrow."

When he came back from the terrace and got into the Sunbeam-Talbot beside her she said:

"If I hadn't been here, what would you have done?"

"Mended the damned thing."

She laughed, and started the engine.

Their talk had been quiet, friendly. Struve's arrest hadn't been mentioned again. Half-way to London he said:

"There's a short cut here, if you want to try it."

She lifted her foot.

"Are you sure?"

"Through East Knoll. Take it fairly slow—the camber's a bit wicked."

The car heeled over slightly, nosing into the narrower road; then she was able to accelerate.

"Where does it come out?"

He said: "You'll recognize the spot. It doesn't save much more than a mile, but it breaks the main road monotony."

The car ran between hedges. Rabbits darted sometimes from the sudden terror of lights.

Her voice was different, less easy.

"Do you take this short cut very often?"

"Sometimes. When I'm in the mood."

"It's narrow. I'd say the main road was better."

"Then I'm sorry I led you astray."

They topped a rise and then curved down between a scatter of barns, black, angular shapes against the faint skyline. In a few minutes he said:

"Pull up here, just for a moment."

She touched the foot brake, turning to look at him. The question was unspoken. He answered it.

"Something I want to show you. It might be interesting." Her left hand moved; the headlights went out.

The car stopped close to the hedge. She looked down at her hands. Their fingers were hooked over the spokes of the steering wheel. Under the black net gloves the knuckles gleamed pale.

His voice was quiet.

"You don't think Struve killed David. Do you?"

She was silent. She didn't look at him. The blood had left her face.

He said in a moment: "This case has been odd. I was involved in Brain's death from the moment it happened. One thing has often got me perplexed. At first I ignored it, then the idea took a hold. Then I began working on it."

He turned his head slightly and looked through the windshield. The road was barely traceable in the faint starlight. "When Brain's car neared mine, down Knoll Hill, his lights dazzled me. They even appeared to reflect against the rear window, because the light in the rear view mirror was blinding me too. For a time, afterwards, I thought there must have been a third car, behind mine; but I'd seen nothing of it when I ran back to the break in the fence. Why hadn't it pulled up, when I did?"

Her voice came painfully.

"Please stop."

As if she hadn't interrupted he said: "I was right. There was a third car. It stood here, at this spot. And the lights in my mirror were these."

He moved his hand. As it touched the switch she caught his wrist. For a second their movements were frozen; then her hand relaxed. The switch clicked as he turned it. The headlights came on. In their beam stood the signpost, reading East Knoll. Beyond it was the curve of Knoll Hill, where the two roads forked. Along the upright posts of the board fence the line of reflectors glimmered crimson against the dark background of the trees.

His voice was unemotional.

"Twice in his life, Brain was trapped in a dazzle of light. Once in his bomber, over France. Again in his Ventura, down that hill. Of a sort, there's poetic justice in what you did."

The silence lasted until she felt she could speak without choking. She was fighting hard not to break down.

"There was justice," she said.

"Of a sort. Your brother was one of the squadron that was wiped out by one man's stupidity, but when Brain came to you—as he came to all their families with his generous confession—you tried to understand him. And you succeeded. Until the issue became mixed up, by Melody—"

"I thought they'd be together in his car—"

"Yes, Pollinger said they were coming down to Beggar's Roost together, didn't he? It's understandable that you thought they'd both be in his car as they reached this danger spot. But accidents happen . . . "

"It wasn't an accident—I'm glad it was only him—"

"Of course. You took him away from Melody, in the only way you could."

She said nothing more. Her hands hung from the wheel, for the moment nerveless. Her face was frozen-looking, her eyes closed. The lashes were moist.

He said quietly: "I'll drive the rest of the way."

He got out. In the distance, his shadow passed along the fence on the hill, enormous as it cut off the twin beams of light. She had moved into the passenger's seat. He climbed in and shut the door.

The gears grated as he shifted the lever.

"Don't let it prey too much on your mind, Sophie. There's only one chance in three you did what you set out to do."

She seemed not to have heard. She sat stiffly beside him with her eyes still closed. He drove away, and the patch of light brightened against the trees as they passed the signpost, turning into the curve of the hill. The reflectors flared red in the dazzle, then darkened one by one as the car drove up the hill, its sound fading among the trees.

22nd

MOVE

BISHOP WAS in his dressing-gown. He had slept for three hours but looked jaded in the strong sunlight that filled the room.

"Gorry?"

"Sherry, please, Hugo."

"Freddie?"

"Same for me, thanks."

Glass clinked musically in the silence.

"Lunch isn't for half an hour," he said to Frisnay over his shoulder. "That'll just about give us time."

Miss Gorringe lit a cigarette, passing Frisnay his drink. He had lost sleep himself, the night before. He moved in his chair until the sunlight was out of his eyes.

Bishop sat down on the davenport.

"Cheers," he murmured.

On the limed-oak desk the Princess Chu Yi-
Hsin sat crouched in the sun, her eyes scarcely open. They widened, sometimes, to the
murmur of their voices, sometimes closed in
brief sleep.

"Struve isn't likely to make any confession,"
said Frisnay in a moment. "He's just closed up
on us."

Bishop said: "Wouldn't you?"

Frisnay grunted. "Anyway, that's all I can tell
you about him. You know the rest. You've something for me?"

"Yes." He took another sip of his drink and
stood up, moving restlessly. "It's very clear-cut
in some ways, Freddie. In every way it's going
to be a headache for someone—possibly for you.
I don't know enough about the law and criminal
proceedings to appreciate what happens when
three independent people murder one man."

Frisnay jerked his head.

"Three!"

"Everett Struve. Melody Carr. Sophie Marsham."

Frisnay watched him with his wide, brown
stare.

"And none of them," said Bishop, "realized that

the others were aiming at the same thing: the death of Brain."

He filled his meershaum from the bowl on the desk, prodding the tobacco down carelessly, his hands moving by habit alone.

"You know all about Struve. It's possible—no more—that when he unhooked the hood latch he killed Brain. All the evidence is in, as much as we're likely to find. With Melody Carr there's no evidence, except for my own word. The same goes for Sophie Marsham. This is the picture. There were two women in love with Brain. Each knew she might lose him to the other. At the end, each felt quite sure she was going to lose him to the other. Melody was certain, because when he went to her flat that night, he went there to say he was going abroad the next morning, to marry Sophie. Sophie was certain, because Brain had promised not to see the other woman again, yet when she was at the bar in Beggar's Roost that night she heard from Pollinger that he was bringing Melody down there to make a night of it. Sophie knew he couldn't do that, the day before their trip to Paris, and still go through with the marriage. And even if he could . . . she wouldn't let him."

He struck a match. The head of the Siamese lifted to watch the flame. Smoke came curling into the sunshine; the cat's eyes followed it, for a moment mesmerized.

Frisnay watched him as he turned away from the desk and began pacing, trying to get the pattern straight in his mind before he put it into words.

"To understand Melody's motive, you've got to understand the woman. I believe I do. If it ever comes round to you to question her, you'll get to know more then than I can possibly tell you now, at second-hand. But don't make any mistake, Freddie. She intended that he should be killed, that night. He was drunk, he was known for his fast driving and his contempt for risk. She challenged him to race her to Beggar's Roost, knowing he'd drive like hell from the minute they started off, and knowing the route took in Knoll Hill—a danger spot at the best of times. She's convinced, at this moment, that she sent him to his death that night. So, to a great extent, am I."

Miss Gorringe was making notes. The dry touch of her pencil over the pad was faintly audible in the room.

Frisnay said: "She's told nobody else about this?"

"I doubt it. I'm nearly certain."

Frisnay gave a nod. Bishop went on:

"Sophie Marsham. She's told me—and Gorry has checked up on most of it—that during the war, Brain lost the squadron of which he was the leader when they were bombing over France. It was a pointless massacre. Brain himself called it 'bloody-mindedness.' After the war, he went to the relatives of the men who had lost their lives, and in an access of self-righteous and hypocritical conscience confessed that their deaths hadn't been necessary, that he was to blame. Among these families was Sophie Marsham. Her brother had been in Brain's squadron. She didn't tell me this, but Gorry found his name last night in a list sent to her by the Air Ministry. Flying Officer George Douglas Marsham, D.F.C."

He waited for a moment, in case Frisnay wanted to put a question. There was no question.

"Sophie was very understanding when Brain made his confession to her. She'd loved her brother, had been broken for a while by his death; but it was war, it was an act of God in a Godless world. She didn't blame David Brain. She met him again, a number of times. Then she fell in love with him. It was mutual. They planned to get married. He told her about Melody; she said break it off. He promised. He didn't break it off. She hung on, keeping her thoughts on the day they'd planned to leave for Paris—Melody couldn't touch them after that.

"But Melody was hanging on, too. It had become a duel of attrition. Each knew the other's power over David, and he himself began being torn apart by the tension: he wanted to go away with Sophie; he couldn't leave Melody." He paused, standing still, thinking. Then: "On that night, Sophie was talking to Pollinger at Beggar's Roost when the phone rang. It was Melody. She said she and Brain were coming down to make a night of it. They were lit up, she added—as one does, sometimes when one's drunk. She rang off. Sophie knew that she'd lost. Brain wasn't seriously considering the Paris trip tomorrow, when tonight he was with Melody. Even the tradition of the champagne-and-good-bye couldn't justify that."

He began walking again. He finished: "Sophie parked her car at the fork on Knoll Hill and waited for the Ventura to come. I believe she had to wait some thirty minutes—she'd left the Roost straight after the phone call and drove in a kind of dull fury to the spot. When the Ventura came down the hill she turned her headlights full on. They struck his windshield, blinding him. Sophie is at the moment convinced she killed Brain." He smiled dryly. "So, to a great extent, am I."

The room was silent. Bishop struck another

match. His hand touched the head of the cat, moving its scalp until it purred.

Frisnay's voice was impatient.

"A lot of this is conjecture, Hugo."

"Yes." He looked at Frisnay. "But it doesn't worry me. I don't think you're very likely to send Struve for trial without first questioning these two women. In fact you daren't, Freddie. I wouldn't let you."

Frisnay got up, standing uncertainly, his glass in his hand. Bishop added:

"Besides, how much is really conjecture? Struve: facts are that he had a motive and that his prints were found on the hood latch of the Ventura. We conjecture only that the cause of the fatal crash was the hood lifting and producing a total black-out of vision at high speed.

"Melody: facts are that she had a motive and that only she spent Brain's last hour on earth with him. We have her word for the fact that she deliberately refused to drive in his car, but challenged him instead to a race. We conjecture only that the cause of the crash was his drunken condition together with the phenomenally high speed he was doing—at her instigation.

"Sophie: the facts are that she had a motive and that when she realized that she hadn't only lost Brain but was being deceived by the man who killed her brother, she left the roadhouse at once and drove to Knoll Hill. All we conjecture is that the cause of the crash was the blinding light that Brain ran into at high speed on a dangerous curve."

He stood looking at Frisnay in silence for a moment before he finished:

"Freddie, I don't know if it's going to be humanly possible to find out what caused Brain's fatal smash. Even I can't say. And I watched it."

Miss Gorringe took Frisnay's empty glass from him and went across to the cabinet. Bishop moved round his desk and looked out of the window. He thought of David Arthur Brain, and for a moment felt sorry for him. Whatever kind of man he had been, life had been loaded against him on that night when he had driven out of London in his car. Three people had tried to kill him. Had only one succeeded? Two? All three? What complicated pattern of circumstances had formed in order to bring him the death they had wanted?

Frisnay's voice came from behind him. Vera Gorringe had given him another sherry. He was staring down at it, saying quietly:

"How many combinations are there, Hugo? Have you gone so far as to total them up?"

Bishop gave a shrug.

"They're practically endless," he said.

Frisnay watched his drink gloomily. He said:

"If he hadn't been drunk, would the lights have killed him, or the speed of his race with Melody, or the black-out made by the hood? Without the lights and the hood, would the drink . . . or the speed . . . ? Without the speed, the lights alone . . . the hood alone . . . ?"

Bishop said gently: "There are even more subtle influences to consider, Freddie; perfectly practical and physical influences. How far—for instance—did the hood fly up? Enough to block the blinding light from Sophie's car? Or only far enough to catch the moth and kill it, giving us a pointer, and not far enough to stop the dazzle of the lights?"

Frisnay drank some of his sherry and spread a left hand in the air. "Thank God," he said, "this isn't my problem, entirely."

"You're going to question these two women?"

He nodded.

"Of course. I have to. And of course I'll have to tell them why. Because you've passed on their confessions to me."

"That's all right. In Melody's case she knew what she was doing. It'll be my word against hers, unless you can trip her somehow. With Sophie, there was no actual confession to me;

343

she simply didn't deny my accusation. You'll find her easier to handle."

Frisnay nodded again, slowly.

"Can I use this, please?"

"Of course."

He picked up the telephone, dialing his office. Bishop talked to Miss Gorringe while Frisnay gave his orders.

"I want two men put on Miss Carr's flat, immediately. I shall be along there in a couple of hours. Two men to keep watch on another woman: Miss Sophie Marsham. She was at the inquest on David Brain, and you can get her address from your——"

"Elton Street," said Vera Gorringe from down the room. "Twenty-five Elton Street."

He repeated the address into the telephone. When he rang off, he leaned back against the edge of the great desk, hands in his pockets, eyes on Bishop.

Bishop said: "I shall be interested to see the outcome of Brain case, Freddie."

Frisnay grunted.

"Good grief, so shall I. A man who's the subject of a coroner's verdict of accidental death has become the victim of murder. Murder intended by three people working independently and ignorant of one another's plans, and successfully achieved by one, two, or all three of them." He shrugged, leaning away from the desk.

Bishop took up the chessmen from the chessboard, standing them one by one in the box. The cat watched him idly. He said:

"It was death in three moves, but which was checkmate?"

He closed the lid and put the box away.

Adam Hall is the pseudonym of Elleston Trevor, the author of over 20 novels. Mr. Trevor resides in Cave Creek, Arizona.